Francesca was brought up in rural Oxfordshire. She gained a PhD in women's literature from Queen Mary, London and practised as a teacher of English for over 25 years. Now semi-retired, Francesca delivers occasional lectures and talks in schools on women's fiction and currently works in her local independent bookshop, a job she loves. This is her first novel. She lives in Hertfordshire with her partner.

This novel is dedicated to my father, Professor Antony de Bono, my mother, Jennifer de Bono, and to my dear friend, Dr Mary Condé…all three much loved and much, much missed.

Francesca de Bono

A DIFFERENT KIND OF SILENCE

To dearest Penny,
with lots of love
and hugs—

AUSTIN MACAULEY PUBLISHERS™

LONDON • CAMBRIDGE • NEW YORK • SHARJAH

A CIP catalogue record for this title is available from the British Library.

ISBN 9781035805006 (Paperback)
ISBN 9781035805013 (ePub e-book)

www.austinmacauley.com

First Published 2024
Austin Macauley Publishers Ltd®
1 Canada Square
Canary Wharf
London
E14 5AA

Thank you to Austin Macauley Publishers for their faith in me. Thank you to my very supportive family, especially my nephew, Patrick, who was among the first to read the novella and to everyone who nodded kindly when I told them how far along I was with the book. A special "thank you" to my best mate, Gill, who trailed around the country with me taking photos and buying endless glasses of wine and to Clara, for her unflagging encouragement. The biggest debt is to my wonderful partner, Sarah, who always had faith I could do it and never once gave me a hard time for taking a year off.

Table of Contents

Preface
The Oxford Times
1st June 2018

The following extracts are taken from the journal found among the private effects of the late Nurse Albertine Gentleman, a long-serving Matron at The Appletrees rest home, formerly Stonehaven, the old rectory at Kirtham. Following the closure of the care home in 1983, the buildings have stood derelict but a movement to conserve the site and restore the original features of the house and gardens has recently begun to gather momentum. Given the Oxfordshire public's growing resistance to new plans to redevelop the plot and the council's intention to bulldoze the main building, Dr Desmond Jackson, Albertine's grandson, has given permission for part of her 1953 diary series to be published.

You can join the petition to conserve the fascinating and historically valuable site of Kirtham Rectory at www.savestonehaven.co.uk.

Monday 20th April

Will I ever feel at home here? I suppose I shouldn't read metaphor into mis-navigation but I got lost again today getting from the library to the dispensing rooms. Much hilarity among the junior staff, as you can imagine. I'm still getting used to Appletrees, such a rambling old place. It's so much bigger than the London clinic and pretty ostentatious for a Christian minister's residence, in my view! Maybe I am over-tired; I've been very busy today. Muriel and Dot have been up to their usual tricks in the public lounge, and I have already had to speak to that new assistant Annie, whom I'm sure is encouraging them. A proper Miss Thing! I do hope I am going to like it here. I am trying to remember why I said yes so readily when Dr Rosenthal recommended me. There seems to be an awful lot to learn, a whole new etiquette with the 'clients' (whatever happened to residents?). On a happier note, tomorrow is my afternoon off. I shall take some time to explore the garden after I've written to Gene*; apparently, there's something called a ginkgo tree on the front lawn which has been here for over a thousand years I'm told. That can't be right, surely?

[*Eugene Jackson, Albertine's fiancé, a mechanic who worked in Oxford prior to their wedding in 1955.]

Wednesday 22nd April

Much more cheerful today. I have made a new friend, who goes by the romantic name of Ambrose East, the gardener and general handyman. He's awfully shabby, not to mention malodorous but he's got a storyteller's twinkle and he's genuinely entertaining. I've noticed him in the grounds before, pottering about in all weathers. He must be all of seventy-five, and I think I detected a touch of glaucoma this afternoon but he retains all his faculties, and then some.

After lunch, I did a loop around the house via the lawns in a bid to reach the copse beyond the church path and promptly found myself stranded, caught in a brief but drenching downpour way on the other side of the fruit cage. Imagine my surprise when what I thought was a heap of old sacking reared up and bundled me into a ramshackle shed beyond the raspberry canes. I tried to remain sparky but it gave me something of a fright; he's a big man, sort of rangy and substantial, the house seemed suddenly very far away. I needn't have worried, he ignored me and made a beeline for his potted geraniums on the soggy window-ledge, billing and cooing to them like a sweetheart. I thought he might have forgotten I was there, balancing with my knees glued together on a rickety wicker chair which has definitely seen better days. Just as I was thinking of sidling out, he wheeled around and rather shyly presented me with half a stale biscuit (oh Lord, what befell the other half?) and some muddy, brown tea, at least I assume that's what it was, which he sloshed out of a pre-war vacuum flask into a grubby plastic beaker. Suppressing a shudder along with my student mnemonic for infectious diseases caused by polluted water ('Cruel, depressing and painful...'), I introduced myself properly and we began to chat.

I have to hand it to him; he's a mine of local information. Here are the best bits, and all delivered without a trace of irony. Prefacing his narrative with a guarantee that this whole place is haunted, he started with what sounded like a belter of a cliché but which I've since found out is actually village lore. Winking theatrically at me, he asked if I'd been up Mollie Minns Lane yet. For an awful moment, I thought he might be referencing some ghastly English euphemism I hadn't come across. Hear this, running parallel to the line of apple trees at the rear of the main house is a path named after a wretched scullery maid who was raped, killed and summarily buried in the garden by one of the clergies who lived here way back along with the Black Death. No kidding! I nearly snorted out my witch's brew. Talk about all the makings of a Hollywood picture. I must remember not to be so flippant in front of Mr East again, though. He fixed me with his rheumy eye and shook his huge, bear-like head so vigorously at what he called 'Hard-headed city folk' that I feared an incipient aneurysm. Anyway, I think I may have upset him. He dried up as quickly as the weather did when he saw my reaction and lumbered off to check the rat traps in the stable block. I'm cross with myself, maybe he had more to say. Mother always said I was precipitate, even before she knew what it meant. If Gene telephones tonight, I must update him; this classic English Gothic stuff is right up his street. Back to work!

Saturday 25th April

Well, that will teach you, Tina Gentleman. I was right about Gene – a dog with a bone in situations like this. I don't know how he does it but people just seem to open up to him. Lubrication might have helped, if I'm cynical. He drove old man East to the Dashwood Arms in the village and was issued with what began to look like the full and unexpurgated version over a pint or two of local Hook Norton. The Mollie Minns thing was just a warm-up for the tourist, as I suspected; I blew it with my scepticism but Gene didn't make the same mistake. While I am inclined to disbelieve it, he has persuaded me otherwise. I have never seen him so visibly shaken and at the same time rather moved by what the old boy shared with him. Apparently, the Easts have dwelt in Kirtham for generations. Mr East's father and grandfather worked here at the Rectory, or Stonehaven as it was called then, as grooms before he was born in 1878 (how about that? He IS seventy-five, my professional eye!). He has seen the house evolve from a stately ecclesiastical residence through all kinds of reincarnations to its present status as a hospice for the elderly. He waxed sentimental, Gene chuckled, about the war years when something called the 'Ox and Bucks' were billeted here in 1914, followed by a visiting regiment of what he called 'Your lot' in '43.'*

[*Ambrose East's casual racism, while being typical of the period, is not endorsed by The Oxford Times. Albertine and Gene were both West Indian. A company of African American airmen were posted temporarily to Upper Heyford Airbase, approximately six miles from Kirtham, in 1944. This may be the erroneous connection Mr East made.]

This is odd. I find myself deliberately avoiding setting down Mr East's spooky recollections. I must admit, something about the tale has affected me deeply. It just sounds so... I don't know, not plausible exactly but sincere and so desperately sad. Here goes, anyway. Gene got the scullery maid tale but pushed for more. Did he have anything else up his sleeve apart from apocryphal local legend? Anything more contemporary that he could perhaps personally verify? At this point, Ambrose (they are firmly on first name terms, these two) cleared his throat, discharging a pellet of silted green tobacco onto the carpet as he jammed on his battered trilby, ready to make off. Gene took the hint, hurried to the bar and got him another pint. The long and short of it is that over the course of the evening the following tender little bombshell was dropped.

In 1896, when Ambrose was just eighteen, he started as a groundsman at Stonehaven, light duties at first, trimming borders and raking gravel. He'd only been working here a year when he first saw her. The way he described it, according to Gene, made the whole experience sound almost unbearably poignant. Certainly, he confessed no sense of horror, perhaps if anything he remains, to this day, oddly proprietorial, protective even. This is how Gene relayed the story, he's such a honey; the nostalgic interpretation has his fingerprints all over it!

It was an early summer's evening, time to knock off, and Ambrose was rinsing his hands at the old Belfast sink beneath the pantry window when he noticed a ladder left propped up against the nursery wall and wandered out to fetch it in. The late afternoon light was buttery against a riot of blossoms and the scene resembled a sentimental painting, a landscape from a golden age in waxy, crepuscular oils. A slight movement, no more than a materialisation of the stillness, drew his eye to a casually meandering figure. It was a young woman. She was simply dressed in a distinctive short wrapper which Ambrose took to be part of a nurse's uniform. The cape, the palest powdery blue – it made him think of a rinsed clean, cold winter sky – was fixed snugly under her freckled chin as if against a bitter wind while down her back snaked a single bright copper braid, like blood from a stubborn wound. As he stared, he realised with a jolt that he could pick out the brickwork of the churchyard wall right through her. She seemed in no hurry, turning and wandering back the way she had come when, quite suddenly, she raised her head and fixed her eyes directly on his own, bottomless, the colour of Christmas trees, he recalled, or deep, deep water. The look she gave him brought a lump to his throat and spoke of unfinished business and a long road ahead. Her expression is the same every time he's caught a glimpse of her, always under the apple trees but not often now there are so many people about. The last time was more than a couple of years ago, on a freezing and foggy November bonfire night, such a heartbreaking smile, stoic, secretive and knowing, a powerful blend of triumph and adversity; the countenance of one to whom everything is lost, and everything won.

Professor Patch Hardcastle advises his daughter, aged ten,
with reference to "The Lady of Shallot"
by Alfred Lord Tennyson

*"Consider Sir Lancelot; did you ever come across a scoundrel
so highly polished? A gleaming shiny shell of a hero if ever I
read of one. All vanity and vacuousness, as hollow as he's
handsome. 'Tirra lirra by the river' indeed. Will any woman
ever hearken to a war cry more blood-curdling? The lady
never stood a chance. Beware the pretty knight, Pauline, it
may be better to remain unrescued in certain circumstances."*

Chapter 1
Autumn 1880, Oxford:
A Funeral;
The Future Contemplated

At last, the swell and hum of departing mourners diminished, rolling along the narrow corridor, tipping out into the porch on a wave of sincere solicitation. For a moment he lingered, watching as they stood huddled under the dripping portico, twittering like starlings mustering for murmuration. Then, as another vicious burst of hailstones skittered against the glass, rattling the leaden window frames, he recoiled involuntarily and stepped away from the window. The day had never properly brightened and now an untimely dusk was approaching. A sly mist had crept in and settled round the honey-coloured Cotswold stone of St John's like fine, suffocating sand. Turning back into the snugly lit library, he could not help reflecting how highly expedient, how almost uncannily timely the sudden death of Oxford's eminent literary luminary, Professor Patrick Hardcastle, had been. Rubbing his hands and suppressing an unseemly smirk, he turned over in his mind his ideas for a few well-chosen words of sympathy to be delivered at High Table after the eulogy tomorrow. Such a terrible loss for the college but what an inspiring legacy, sic transit gloria and after all, the Lord giveth in order that he must take away, too. Spontaneous self-congratulation yet again put an end to his musings but well, really, it was the very least he could do, wasn't it? Why just the other day the good Professor had been confessing, confidentially of course, his concerns about the uncertain marital fate of his cherished only daughter and wishing the days of gallantry hadn't vanished along with the original manuscripts of Sir Thomas Malory.

As far as Aubrey Tertius Kite was concerned, his role as curate of St Giles, the modest church crouched at the junction of Oxford's Woodstock and Banbury Roads was already proving tedious. It once incorporated a whiff of both incentive and allure, given the potentially delicate hand he had been dealt but he was an accomplished player and he had mastered the game easily with his usual trumps of calculation and charisma; he was now regarded as something of a local treasure and guaranteed access to polite society. He had positively relished the thirsty whispers about his eligibility for he was a more than averagely appealing prospect. Tall, vigorous and athletic, with a sensual mouth and slim, feminine fingers, on entering the clergy Kite had retained his rich, blue-black mutton chop whiskers, which he cherished with a vanity just this side of decency. He had ruminated long and hard about the finishing touch to his ecclesiastical persona, finally selecting a pair of fine, thin gold rimless spectacles. The curate's vision was of the very sharpest and penetrating clarity but he had long considered a conspicuous public flaw necessary the better to evoke sympathy, especially among the more susceptible females of his flock. His wide apart eyes were storm-cloud, steely grey, fetching and intelligent. Something of a frustrated dandy, Kite dared not forego his dog-collar but consoled himself with an enviable collection of the finest Chinese silk handkerchiefs, fragrant and effulgent, which he draped with artful nonchalance from the pocket of his sombre coat; canary yellow, Amaranth pink, episcopal purple, depending on his humour.

As he settled into his new position, he pictured himself as a bridge, a conduit spanning art and commerce: the papery academics nestling inviolable in their musty libraries and the newly rich merchant classes clattering into the city from the industrial north. He would simply place himself at the metaphorical confluence at which the wealth was counted, preach a few judicious words about almsgiving and the afterlife, and settle back to enjoy himself. But that was then. Now, like a mongoose in a menagerie, he knew every stinking inch of his hutch and even the view beyond the bars was just so very... parochial. Perhaps this latest acquisition would go some way to boosting his lofty aspirations. There'd been some early talk of two of Hardcastle's more pertinacious academic colleagues being granted guardianship of both Pauline and her younger brother Linus but they had been outmanoeuvred by his assurance to the ailing professor that he would honour his promise to marry his daughter at the first opportunity if she would have him, sir. The latter part was mere courtesy, naturally; he would brook no refusal in a gambit which would deliver the final polish to his already sparkling renown as a churchman so philanthropic that the archbishop himself would be forced to acknowledge it. Such an unparalleled act of Christian charity; a marriage and, he grudgingly supposed some kind of improvised adoption, in one magnanimous gesture. And then, surely, he could legitimately petition for a larger residence, a country position perhaps, as befitting his young household.

Not that it had been uncomplicated, he admitted to himself in a rare moment of candour. Blather and Bumptious had been part of the Professor's entourage long before Kite himself had arrived in Oxford. Ten years ago, when the premature death of Mrs Hardcastle threatened the imminent implosion of family, they had supported their heartbroken friend with the utmost fealty, discharging their duties as godparents to his two children with expediency and discretion. Ever since, the professor had retained them as his closest confidants. Later, they made no attempt to disguise their mistrust of the flamboyant new curate and had been known to express collective suspicion at what they considered to be Kite's tactical campaign to inveigle his way into any kind of favour. But this was before he, a confirmed heretic as far as the creed of romantic love was concerned, had noted for himself Pauline's startling pre-Raphaelite beauty at their first encounter outside his church that bright Easter Day. Come to think of it, she and her little brother were flanked even then by their academic watchdogs, whom she had introduced quietly as Mr Barnaby from the Faculty of Law and Dr Belshire of Medicine.

The former stood with the erect carriage of an overzealous footman; he was thin to the point of emaciation, hawkish, with sooty, ink-stained cuffs, a pencil permanently wedged behind his right ear and an absurdly glamorous goatee which shone like Whitby jet. Undeniably eloquent, he practised the unsettling habit of looking just above one's eyeline during his addresses, a ruse perfected as a long-serving barrister at

Lincoln's Inn. His associate, bark to Barnaby's bite, was the more rakish of the pair, in a balding frock coat of raspberry velvet and clashing scarlet suspenders. A Regency anachronism, with grizzled hair the colour of cobwebs, fixed in a queue by a silver bow, Belshire's muscular frame moved with a natural swagger, despite his sixtieth decade being well advanced. The two were never seen apart, and while Kite found highly provoking Belshire's habit of completing Barnaby's sentences, a quirk which seemed only to strengthen their bond, he still found himself occasionally envious of their steadfast mutual society. Even they could not fail to be impressed by the strategic elegance of his opening comment to Professor Hardcastle that first Sunday. An invitation to sherry duly followed his seemingly spontaneous admiration for the poetry of the curate Hopkins, recently departed from neighbouring St Aloysius. And all this from one judicially seasonal quotation, "Nothing is so beautiful as Spring". They didn't need to know about the spark of jealousy which flared every time he glimpsed a band of his Dominican brothers, sleek as magpies in their black and white robes and always at peace at the doors of The Oratory.

As if invoked by some manner of spell, at that very moment a smouldering shard slipped from the fire, picking up speed as it bounced across the worn Turkey rug before coming to rest against his boot. For a second, he simply stared, fascinated, even as the residual heat began to pulse through his toes and a charred black hole mushroomed through the lapis-coloured wool. A low cry at his elbow roused him from his reverie and instantly he registered pain along with an unexpected sense of alarm. "Oh sir, please! It was father's favourite. I couldn't bear it to be spoiled and I would so like

23

to take it with us… with your permission." Still, he remained fixed to the spot, riven by a sudden presentiment of disaster so total, so sweeping that he was forced to grip the marble mantel and close his eyes for a second. Quick as a flash, she tipped the burning ember onto the toe of her calfskin shoe and flipped it back into the grate where it spat satisfyingly and settled at last. He couldn't look at her. "Have a care, woman, have a care. I make the decisions now. And don't call me sir if there are people still about, for goodness' sake, we are engaged after all." Still shaken, swiping at the ginger tom just settling comfortably into an upholstered wing-back, he flung himself on the sofa by the fireside, swinging his throbbing foot onto its faded arm and raising his voice against the cat's indignant yowling. "I haven't settled on the furniture from this room; I have some decisions yet to make about what to sell. Remember what the Bible says about possessions, Pauline, they are temporary." He regarded her coldly over his glasses. "For we brought nothing into this world, and it is certain we can carry nothing out. And that creature will have to go too; I won't have pets at number 45. Oh, do stop snivelling, and fetch me another Madeira. Quickly now!"

His earlier satisfaction fled, Aubrey Kite fought the suspicion, not for the first time, that he was doomed to live a disappointed man. Born into genteel obscurity in Birmingham, the only son of a decent and assiduous industrialist, Kite's had been a swift, ignominious and unoriginal (as far as sin went) undoing. Too early in his boisterous youth virtue, persistently slackening from its moorings, was soon cut loose and he was forced to seek shelter and at least a show of respectability in the clergy as a potentially inflammatory scandal was dismantled. In his opinion, his family's concerns were exaggerated. Things had come to what he considered a highly expedient conclusion; the principal witness in no position to testify and the injured party generously compensated into long-term discretion. Nevertheless, his mother's stepbrother, Colonel Sir Antony Amey, a powerful Oxfordshire landowner with the ear of the ailing Prime Minister, no less, had secured for him this local curate's position, in return for what Kite considered to be downright slavish compliance. What had disturbed his conservative uncle, the words "deviant" and "perverse" had been murmured sotto voce, Kite had judged at the time as merely piquant. But what real choice did he have? He was painfully aware that his billet here constituted what the old soldier had wincingly defined as a period of trial and long overdue adjustment; he was never naïve enough to assume that his benefactor granted him any kind of independence or autonomy along with the keys to St Giles. His unassuming house of worship was owned by St John's College, and Sir Amey had been only too crassly specific about the size of the 'Anonymous' donation needed to secure their reluctant acquiescence. Momentarily discomfited, he recalled their final encounter; words were discharged by both sides but never so accurately as the Colonel's summation that Kite was certainly pretty enough but too bloody spineless for the military and that he had better damned well develop a vocation other than that of self-promotion. He had closed with a blistering salvo about manipulation and deceit being the very poorest weapons in a gentleman's armoury. The narrow terms of his patronage merely served to whet Kite's naturally prodigious appetite.

Betrothal had done nothing to repair the adverse camber of the curate's heart or soothe his recurrent resentments. Since climbing out of his uncle's carriage two years ago envy had dripped into his days and down the back of his neck like pestilential drizzle. His first, he now realised callow assumption, was that the rather dignified Old Parsonage would offer him some solace as his natural seat, given his new status. Instead, he was installed at number 45 St Giles, a red-brick terraced upright, with a black wrought-iron balcony and a rear garden which bristled with concentric circles of evergreen box and blue rosemary. Its high walls ensured a fragrant privacy and Kite had grudgingly developed a relish of enclosed spaces and the freedom they afforded away from prying North Oxford eyes. Unfortunately, his one resident servant, young Clara Pebble, squint-eyed and pigeon-toed, offered no temptation of consolation there, for he liked to think he retained his standards. He only lacked the final endorsement from his fawning congregation (mostly matrons and widows, his favourite demographic, the one well-fed, the other well-heeled) to the archbishop in order to advance his project, a condition guaranteed by his impending wedding and its opportunity for communal celebration. His greatest achievements he felt were yet to come; celebrity and recognition, along with all the attendant material trimmings, were just over the near horizon.

Ten miles away, to be exact. Kite had first set eyes on Stonehaven, the Rectory at Kirtham when he accompanied the Bishop of Oxford to deliver a Lent sermon to local parishioners early in his tenure. The deceptively self-effacing rural village suggested itself as a perfect refuge from what he was beginning to regard as bourgeois collegiate banality.

26

Stonehaven was spacious and impressive, with sweeping gardens laid to lawn and a wide parterre splashed by the afternoon sun. No backwater, the village boasted its own mansion inhabited by a Baronet and his line, along with magnificent parklands that lured many a visiting dignitary. The vicar attached to Kirtham would necessarily preside over the Akeman Benefice, no fewer than seven associated churches, the beginnings of an empire. That day, the bishop and the rector, the latter a portly tortoise with a squashed damson for a nose and a pronounced gouty limp, had raucously compared the potency of the fine claret at Kirtham Park with the robust home brew afforded by the rowdy annual village feast of Lamb Ale on Trinity Sunday. From then on, he had worked harder on his game plan; currently a sprat in a stagnant bilge, he aspired to be feted a much more sizeable fish in a clear, cool country brook.

For the curate was daily gaining confidence that he could reclaim his own destiny; the future would be of his choosing, not part of a humiliating renegotiation among his kinsmen. To play his next gambit, he had been obliged to find a wife, if only to take his legitimate joy where he might. Professor Hardcastle's daughter had been named, according to her doting father, after Robert Browning's poetic musing on reason versus instinct and it afforded Kite some prurient amusement to speculate on the old man's choice when he was forced to yield to one or the other at her conception. Pauline would do well as a churchman's wife, her attractions lent themselves to the sacred, his very own Vespertina Quies as suggested by Mr Burne-Jones. Her virtuous modesty both thrilled and excited him. She was a little closed up yet and cleverer than he would have liked; shy, bookish, with rust-red tresses tamed tight under a bonnet and milky skin splashed with ribbons of freckles which massed and muddled over her clavicles, sliding maddeningly down the back of her neck and under her shawl. She had acquiesced to his proposal without a word, as he knew she must, just a shallow, pretty nod and the softest of exhalations.

Sighing deeply himself, Kite remembered he was not alone and glanced over at her silhouette, statue-like against the drizzled pane. Her burnished head was low but a gentle sobbing persisted. Instinctively, he drew his kerchief from his pocket almost at the same time registering it as his favourite – an intricate paisley in pale greens and golds, far too bonny for blubber. "Not so comely now," he muttered aloud coldly. The evening stretched ahead with only John Gower's Confessio Amantis offering any form of diversion. He could play at churchman all his life, but nothing would change his mind: physical over divine love would always be his preference. Resolved, he shouldered past Pauline, seizing his hat and coat. His last, more careful action was to obscure the streak of white at his throat with a long woollen scarf before dousing the lights and seeking sanctuary in The Gardener's Arms. His bride, he consigned to the dark.

Professor Patch Hardcastle consults his daughter, aged
seventeen, with reference to "Measure for Measure"
by William Shakespeare

*"The triumphant Vincentio has restored order to corrupt
Vienna, lavishly dispensing mercy among his subjects
throughout the final scene. Some are granted the weddings of
which they always dreamed, some confined to a lifetime's
penury by the very same rite. Is marriage the ultimate reward
or the direst of punishments, asks the Bard. Before the curtain
falls, the final declaration is issued; will Isabella do her Duke
the honour of becoming his bride? Like so many proposals, it
isn't really a question, merely a proclamation of possession,
a public decree of ownership.*

*"Her reply echoes through dramatic history – silence, but
defiant or acquiescent? Happy ever after or not, what do you
think, Pauline?"*

Chapter 2
Spring 1881, Oxford:
A Wedding; A Past Remembered

When she was twelve, Pauline had made her regular dawn pilgrimage out onto the narrow balcony which boasted a view across the college quad. Despite her father's half-hearted attempts at chastisement – "You'll be sorry when bats swoop into your room and start nesting in your hair while you're asleep, Miss!" – It had become her custom to leave scraps for the songbirds there. She was on good terms with Oxford's plentiful and dedicated forager pigeons, too often the beneficiaries of her largesse, and the ritual afforded her precious encounters with friendly robins and once a duet of sprightly sparrows who perched beside her for a full five minutes, trilling a thank you very much. That morning, though, was different, a razor-sharp, bright sunlight sliced through the air, bouncing blindly off the brickwork while a nimble, whistling wind played the railings like a harp. The discovery she had made caused her to drop soundlessly to her knees, grazing skin and drawing blood. An eviscerated and lop-legged blackbird was draped obscenely between the iron palings. The grotesque tableau was hypnotic in its horror; she bent close, the tiny creature's clotted chest fluttering as it appeared to contemplate the sheer drop beneath its dangling head. Within seconds, the bird had died but its fate was branded on her childish brain. She had witnessed in that elongated minute dulling eyes registering their own doom; the cruel irony of a fatal fall where once flight had been, liberty irreversibly revoked. Her father had padded out, shepherding her back inside while he dealt discreetly with the delicate remains but there was no such mercy for her now. She would never bring herself to blame him; he had believed in Kite's integrity because he believed in everyone's. What use to argue faith abused or gullibility exploited? To whom should she complain? Like the blackbird, her mute scream would never be loud enough to wake the household. Atrophy was all that was left, the unnatural finality of stasis.

Seated by an open window with her sketch pad, Pauline only realised she was weeping again when smoky charcoal tributaries began to deface her drawing – a wretched collared dove, tight around its throat a monstrous, shining band of gold. In less than a week, she would be Mrs Kite. The elderly maiden aunt with whom she and Linus had been lodging in Headington could barely contain her excitement but for her, events had become torturous, especially since giving up the college rooms that had been her home for so long. It was the spring following Father's death and though the weather was clement, it seemed to Pauline that a biblical storm continued to rage, prostrating and crippling in its intensity, riding the axis of her days, bespoke and inexhaustible. The sheer scale of the destruction brought about by his absence from her life could not be quantified; she literally struggled to breathe at times, the dull, perpetual ache in her chest thickening without warning into a volley of punches from a pugilist's fist. Colours were muted or too intense, sounds muffled or over-shrill. She had lost her equilibrium, she feared forever. Her father's passing had condemned her to a newly refracted world, nauseating like seasickness and permanently off-kilter, a place she could no longer navigate. Days were spent either prone, laid low with lethargy or worse, spinning, driven and manic; grief exhausted her.

She had gulped down stories about him in the days after his passing as if to slake a desert thirst. According to his friends, Patch Hardcastle had stooped even at eighteen, bent over his beloved books until someone straightened him up for a meal or to go to bed. They recollected his daily attire of motley socks and trailing ties; he had been known to wear two jackets at a time to facilitate the stuffing of numerous pockets with small scraps of densely written notes. At the varsity, he had scintillated, both as a student and a don, no wonder he had retained an honorary teaching position up until his death, along with a pension and a gratis residence. Affectionate, academically gifted and utterly hopeless in the world outside the college walls, the Professor was quick to laughter like a breaking dam; his was the most memorable of mobile faces, crumpled and deeply seamed, quick hazel eyes retracting into two crescent moons at some perceived witticism. So romantic that he had married late, for love, at fifty-one despite the fact, they recalled fondly, that he had never mastered responsibility of any practical, financial or domestic kind. Frequently, his associates Messrs Barnaby and Belshire had been dispatched from college to avert disaster, like eventually tracking her down at the Ashmolean Museum after closing time when she was ten years old because her father had wandered off to deliver an evening lecture on John Milton, did she remember? Samson Agonistes, wasn't it? And what about when he rigged out his toddler son in a homemade cap and gown so that he could accompany him to High Table because he thought he might be able to hold his own among the dons? Best of all was the highly credible college rumour that Patch had attempted to broker peace singlehandedly between Thackeray and Dickens at The Garrick Club before settling into a semi-friendly dispute with the latter about the implications for women of Dora Spenlow, whom he labelled 'capitulation personified'. In the first few miserable weeks, his daughter fretted that she could only picture him wiry and enquiring in old age, with unruly wisps of ginger hair protruding from an ancient Afghan fez stiff with orange cat hair; a dandelion clock blown hard through the middle. His life's work had been the exhaustive study of the happy ending, which he acknowledged an essential tautology. The laudatory obituary in The Times suggested that he had secured his holy grail, dying peacefully in his sleep at home at the age of seventy but Pauline would never concur, not while her heart was a haemorrhage of anguish.

Later, she found solace browsing through a jumble of happy childhood memories, when she and her father had been inseparable explorers, devouring the city with hungry eyes and hopeful hearts. She was the perfect companion, he had always asserted, unflagging and receptive but also slow to fear and open to adventure. Together they raced around the perimeter of Wellington Square, pressing their faces against the balustrade as they counted the starlings yelling in their leafy green fiefdom. They pondered the flying stone angels reclining on the buttered scone turret of the Radcliffe

Observatory, agreeing that they fared less favourably than the magnificent, knotted Triton guarding the Infirmary. She was taught to identify Hawksmoor as they sized up the Oxford University Press building, even though she secretly preferred the frivolous French Chateau of Pitt Rivers. Her favourite forays were into the rattle and clatter of the covered market where the stink of the farmyard met the kaleidoscope of the flower garden: the greengrocer's looping falsetto, the brilliant smile of the African girl scooping cobnuts from a tipped sack, swine heads grimacing on the butcher's slab as swinging pheasants flashed turquoise in the doorways. Her mother would insist on accompanying them further afield, packing savouries for their expeditions to Wytham Woods or to Port Meadow to scout for kingfishers. They would come home exhausted but exhilarated, her father always settling down to study, no matter how long the day had proved; the incessant clink in the rigging of his mind was the ambient music of her early years and she missed it terribly, along with the custom of stories at bedtime. Literature was her father's gold. "It's more than make-believe, Paulie, it's a mappa mundi. A tonic or a toxin, the written word is a perfect prism through which shines the human condition in all its ugly majesty!"

More recently, she had learned to conjure him at will, just too far for touch or talk but close enough for crumbs of comfort when desolation threatened to overwhelm her. St John's had been thrilled with the bequest of his books and writings, genuinely effusive in the dispensation of sympathy and gratitude in equal measure. The rest of his possessions had been so swiftly portioned, parcelled and packaged that she had scarcely registered it. She retained a few keepsakes – a pair of mahogany bookends in the form of rearing bears

34

accompanied her to St Giles, they had lost a front paw a piece but their defiant posture heartened her – and some of the better items of furniture. His beloved hat she had lowered gently into his grave along with the last two stanzas of Thomas Gray's Elegy, according to his wish. And thus, his brim-full and cluttered life was tidied away in the course of a single afternoon, leaving behind two empty-hearted orphans whose lives had barely begun. Now here she was, just turned twenty and imminently a cleric's wife. It didn't seem to matter that she barely knew Mr Kite (she couldn't call him Aubrey, it was too intimate). That his good looks and sacred profession had somehow serendipitously combined to grant him the most intimate access to her had provoked a spike of alarm which was quickly blunted by the realisation that her unmarried status had wedged the door wide open. Her brother, blithe in his ten-year-old world, had solemnly admitted that he found great consolation in the match, for surely it meant that their dear father would be nearer to them daily if they spent more time in a churchyard? She shook her head regretfully as she recalled her father's analysis of Tennyson's hero, with his 'coal-black curls' and his sycophantic song. How like Father, not to recognise in real life the lesson that his beloved literature had taught him. And after that it been simple; her father had grown weak with worry, and she found herself in a position to soothe his disquiet. While it could never be a love match, a semblance of security must suffice.

The preparations for the wedding, a far more pretentious affair than she would have liked, were further cause for dejection. Her affianced had insisted on showy ornamentation, authorising a garish spray of pink silk roses to be embroidered onto the bodice of her simple Lawn dress. An elaborate matching veil managed both to obscure and to smother, her mother's unassuming lace having been dismissed as ludicrously outmoded. When a jubilant St John's offered to pay for the breakfast as well as her costume, it was as if the final stitch had been sewn into her pastel shroud. Was it farce or was it tragedy when the luckless maid, ordered by Kite to buy orange blossom, had returned with armfuls of lily-of-the-valley instead? Pauline alone knew that these pretty little snowbells were as toxic as digitalis, an omen which only served to stoke her disquiet.

Of the ceremony itself, she retained only ragged recollections. A flicker of warmth as she spotted Linus, sailor suit-smart with a straw boater amongst the crowd flanking the gangway; he'd been bookended by Mr Barnaby and Dr Belshire in matching sombre expressions. The bells tolling tipsily through the spice-scented Lady Chapel. Clara Pebble with doleful mien hunkered in the back pew. The long walk back down the aisle subjected to such blatantly intrusive examination that it made her skin itch. Outside, the sky had brindled, and the air cooled. No one gave it a second thought when, halfway through the feast, she rubbed her little brother's chocolate-covered mouth with her new husband's chequered handkerchief but under the table the broadly smiling groom had pressed his index finger into the soft flesh of her thigh, exerting pressure until she had nearly swooned from the pain. Mid-afternoon saw them back at the house, where an overexcited Linus was confined to bed and the curate wasted no time establishing his new and brutal government. The contract between them was unambiguously prescriptive; Pauline would suffer for every perceived transgression, however trifling. She was to speak when spoken to unless to provide affirmation or corroboration and if he asked her, the answer would always be yes.

Before her brother had succumbed to sleep, she surrendered her virginity wordlessly amongst the tangled leafy whorls behind the house. The pale skin of her lower back had been striped with livid lacerations for days afterwards, worthy stigmata, he'd suggested, for the begetting of an heir. And so, married life began. Never naturally garrulous, she grew reclusive, only forcing herself to stay cheerful around Linus as they raised plants together in the sunny kitchen, sharing in his euphoria when mint burgeoned extravagantly overnight or the scent of thyme wafted through the house, turning the passageways into Tuscany. She reminded him how their mother used to say that if herbs could sing, then all five senses would be rewarded by their husbandry.

Occasionally, she was called upon to entertain her husband's acquaintances, the Deacon on a teatime visit, a grandee from Kirtham dropping in for a sherry, a dowager requiring a consultation about an overdue headstone. At these events, her husband would invariably speak for her, inspiring guests unanimously to admire her demure piety. These experiences challenged her profoundly and called for every ounce of deference she could muster. Once, after she had inadvertently interrupted a quarrel between Kite and an angry relative, he had calmly extinguished his cigar on the back of her hand and she was obliged to wear gloves for a fortnight. The sequence and design of her days were patterned by pain and the scrupulous avoidance of it; she learned to keep her opinions to herself, he would merely oppose them as a matter of course. Grief for her father was something he would not tolerate; sentimentality of any kind had no place in his world. He saw slights everywhere, too arbitrary to predict. When he was convinced that he discerned his caricature in her rendition of a disgruntled heron, the ensuing twisted wrist and destruction of her sketch books forced her to admit vulnerability, but still she refused to accommodate fear.

Instead, she acknowledged that her cherished relationship with her younger brother, necessarily her dearest asset, must harden into a more dispassionate one. Thus far, she had successfully concealed all evidence of abuse and Linus remained oblivious, by design. Sometimes the strain of deception stung more than her wounds. She suspected that he was Kite's insurance, a tool to preserve her passivity; the ghastly truth was that her brother was only safe as long as she was not. The only way she could protect Linus was by relinquishing him. Recently, she had overheard a plan to enrol him in a famous naval school in the capital, a scheme which ignited within her equal measures of hope and misery.

Her meditations were disturbed by the silent arrival of Clara Pebble, eyes down and frown firm: "Yes? What is it, Clara?" she prompted gently. The girl was always so uncomfortable, as if she didn't fit into her own skin. All angles and sharp surfaces, her cheekbones were scattered with scars and her sullen mouth drooped. The artist in Pauline had once or twice had to suppress the ready analogy that her eyes really were like two dark chips of gravel in the sloped escarpment of her face. She was always kind to her, Linus appeared to be very fond of her, but their relationship never progressed beyond the stiffly formal and she continued to inspire in her mistress a sad sort of surprise, like a doll left out in the rain or a snowdrop in summer. "Message from Sir, a reminder about dinner at Kirtham Park tonight. You've got to wear your green, he says… Madam", she bobbed out. Pauline blanched at the mention of the grand house, which they had visited just once before at the behest of the bishop, who was seeking a new incumbent at the parish and required the approval of the baronet. On their way home in the Dashwood's brougham her husband had dragged his tie pin deep along the length of her calf in return for what he judged lukewarm attentions paid to the rector. Tonight, he had already ordered her to lay out the off-the-shoulder ivy satin, ludicrous against the chill of the April evening. No doubt the travelling rug would be denied her again so as to keep her complexion fresh. The only thing she could recall of the imposing residence was a wood panel engraving by Grinling Gibbons in the entrance hall depicting a distorted vast heap of dead game, flattened carcasses of fish coiled about with wilting grouse. It had struck her as suitably sacrificial as she was led into the drawing-room. But she must rouse herself, lest Clara too suffer the consequences of Kite's impatience. She would reconsider her brother's future tomorrow but tonight she must dissemble and debase herself in the name of social advancement.

From "Brother and Sister"
by George Eliot

School parted us; we never found again
That childish world where our two spirits mingled
Like scents from varying rose that remain
One sweetness, nor can evermore be singled.
Yet the twin habit of that early time
Lingered for long about the heart and tongue:
We had been natives of one happy clime
And its dear accents to our utterance clung.

Chapter 3
Summer 1882, Oxford:
Mother Recalled; Brother Lost

While vertiginously romantic, Clara Pebble was not a wicked girl and she remonstrated with herself daily about her debilitating hatred of Mrs Kite. It wasn't manifest but beneath her remarkably unpropitious features there beat a heart of pumice. Sure, the woman hadn't done a thing wrong other than be married to the object of Clara's affections and it wasn't fair to blame her, but so patent an underestimation of her blinding good fortune meant that by the time she'd cleared the breakfast things she was puffed up with antipathy all over again. For if the maid was like a candle waiting to be lit, it was her great misfortune that she had fallen incandescently in love with Kite the moment she had first answered the door to him. His classical features and brooding gaze had converted her completely and ever since he had become her true calling. Every morning, she laid a furtive kiss on the rim of his cup on her way to the parlour and when he left the house she would scurry over to his still-warm chair and languish there immodestly until her chores called her below stairs. Her most fervent prayer was to attend morning service at St Giles to hear him preach, for her a longing that transcended the religious. However, filial obligation demanded that she spend Sunday mornings with her widowed mother on Osney Island in a canal-side cottage with the exact dimensions of a damp punt. Ever since her father had been scooped from the stinking water beneath the steps of The Waterman's Arms, ropes cast like winding sheets about his waterlogged body but half a mile from home, she had taken it upon herself to go into service to better observe the etiquette and appetites of the gentry. Not blessed with natural buoyancy, a career among the navvies had always seemed a fearful option and besides, Clara Pebble's ultimate objective was employment in a teashop in town, knee-deep in nothing more noxious than fragrant Oolong. What was left of her heart she gave to Linus Hardcastle with his thatch of flaxen hair and dimpled grin. Thus far, she had remained unobtrusive at number 45 but he had quickly learned that she was a soft touch for an extra macaroon. Tasked weekly with buying blooms for the house, and still picking up the rudiments of seasonal floristry, Clara had settled on scabious, or maybe speedwell to describe the boy's eyes; she was nothing if not fanciful in her drudgery. Pausing her dusting of the picture frames, she squinted out of the French windows and caught sight of Madam, dozing on the lawn while her brother tinkered with his toys. Later she would bring out some lemonade for the child but before that she would take advantage of uncommon privacy to ascend the stairs and shake out the curate's pillows again.

Pauline, prone among the layered shadows of the hedges was dreaming fitfully of her mother, whom she recalled in snatches, like balm on a bramble scratch, scraps and slithers of images prompted by sounds or colours. When you couldn't remember, what that as bad as forgetting? Even after all this time, the involuntary grip and sting of her memory lingered. Mrs Beatrice Hardcastle, nicknamed Birdie by her besotted husband, had died at Linus' birth when Pauline was nine and she had only endured it because her mother had expressly instructed her to do so and there was no one she adored, respected and trusted more. Dr Belshire had been gentle but definitive in his warning that her condition was more than precarious and yet she had never once wavered, gently taking Pauline aside and making her promise to love her father enough for the both of them. She had gripped her hand so hard that her fingernails left four upturned smiles imprinted in her daughter's palm. "You, your father, me and your brother, very soon." She came of Scandinavian stock, with thick, strawberry blonde hair and misty blue eyes. Sharp, inquisitive, elegant and good-humoured, Ma was fond of jokes, jelly and gin. Her temper was legendary; she was just as quick to have it out as to make it up. Her clothing was colourful and eccentric, men's jackets, exotic kaftans and a penchant for purple and green, the brighter the better. She revered the English countryside and would often delight her daughter by bursting into a tuneful rendition of William Blake's "Green and Pleasant Land" at the top of her voice, especially in company. Birdie had famously walked Offa's Dyke and Hadrian's Wall alone and unaided, unheard of for the time. Her passion was for standing stones, burial mounds and tors. She had coaxed Patch into hiring a Hansom cab from Oxford all the way out to the Rollrights on the Warwickshire border, a thrilling enterprise which saw the three of them stranded overnight at a roadside inn, trapped by sudden snowfall. "Love is a stone circle," she pronounced, suddenly serious, "unbreakable." Christmases and birthdays were spent outdoors with shovels, chunks of cake and mugs of chocolate. Her mother's funeral had dawned almost unbearably sunny, a celebratory air had permeated the morning like incense, crowds of admirers enjoying weather sent by the angels to take back one of their own. But for the exquisite misery afforded by the prior notice of her death, Patch Hardcastle would have succumbed to his sorrow. His eulogy was characteristically eloquent, and while he alluded to himself as sheered down the middle, an Ozymandias with sand in his eyes, he learned from that fateful day to manage what he understood to be a noble disability, an honourable amputation; Birdie lived on in Pauline and in Linus, just as she swore she would. In her daughter's dreams, her mother was always laughing, reciting some fascinating historical circumstance while drinking boiling tea straight from the pot.

Outside on the hot flags, a song thrush was battering a snail. Its beak had skewered a portion of emerging meat and as it danced lightly about, gaining purchase at every shift, its head whipped from side to side, thrashing the shell repeatedly on the stone, raising dust as it repositioned itself for a fresh assault. Downstairs again, Clara was fascinated by the sheer disparity of the odds, the single-minded savagery beaten out audibly in the July sunshine, its cruel dénouement inevitable. By the time she had pulled herself together and sprinted out into the garden, the bird had flown and the mosaic of scattered shards told their own story.

Of Linus, there was no sign aside from his discarded skipping rope, spiralled around a wooden puppet in a method all too reminiscent of her poor old Da. A rudimentary search of the paving stones and lawn advanced no clues, and she was forced to deposit the tray back inside before she could extend her explorations. Clara's better judgement advised her to rouse Mrs Kite to enlist her help, if only to avoid accusations of negligence later. Her mistress was lying recumbent on the soft grass, her left arm flung above her head and her right resting lightly on her chest. She had been browsing a slim pamphlet of poetry; Clara could only make out a foreign-looking name that suggested a rose. The pages had blown across her cheek as she slept and as Clara bent to retrieve the book, she realised with a start that Madam's face was marked with a garish streak, an angry blaze of sunburnt flesh, like half of a permanent blush. Appalled, she turned away again, unable to summon the words necessary to communicate such a blight for something had caught her eye by the base of the wall at garden's far perimeter, a glint of poppy-red enamel paint: Linus' favourite spinning top. Crashing through the purple maze, Clara plunged into the furthest of the prickly hedges, emitting an animal shriek as the barbs pierced her skin. By the time Pauline had joined her, she was bawling unrestrainedly and pointing with a trembling finger at Linus, lodged apparently lifeless beneath a flowering rosemary bush of almost unspeakable loveliness.

Instantly, time took on an air both magical and sadistic. Clara sped away to summon first Dr Manley from his Pusey Street practice and then the curate from St Giles. Pauline, ashen and stricken with guilt, stayed beside Linus, who was barely breathing. Her brother's cherubic face was distended, his lips blue. He lay in a foetal position, curled up like a periwinkle among the mauve blossoms as if he had decided to snatch a scented nap. One of his small hands was clenched and she struggled to prise his fingers apart only to find a lean and malevolent wasp nestled there, intact and airborne within seconds. The sun slunk behind a solitary cloud as Dr Manley pottered across the lawn, hitching up his trousers and complaining loudly about the interruption to his lunch. The shuffling, aged medic brought with him a whiff of formaldehyde and a pessimistic outlook, scratching his papery chin as he warbled words at her that sounded like they came from underwater, each term more terrifying than its predecessor; anaphylactic shock, incipient cyanosis, the possibility of laryngeal edema, always a risk of acute pulmonary emphysema. Lucky the child was a decent weight and in good health, he'd do what he could for him. By the time Kite arrived home, vexed at the disturbance and only vaguely curious, Linus was on his way to the Infirmary on a makeshift stretcher, with the tearful maid hiccupping along beside it. Pauline was too distraught to accompany them. Fervently hoping the military school's deposit could be recovered, Kite encouraged himself to remains sanguine: Linus' death or his recovery would result in permanent expulsion either way. To extend a naval metaphor, it was time to clear the decks so that he could concentrate on furthering his own family line, let alone supporting another man's. Having made the right public noises about his wife's temporary facial disfigurement, back in the privacy of her room he joked sardonically that she was his very own Hester Prynne but without the relish for recreation. Thereafter, despite the lateness of the hour, he beat a hasty retreat to his office attached to the church, pleading paperwork.

In reality, Kite was making for George Street and the New Theatre, outside which there loitered an off-the-books climbing boy so filthy and so feral that he was nicknamed the human ferret; there was nothing he couldn't unearth, no site he couldn't penetrate. More accurately, he was a sturdy pit pony of a youth, with startlingly protuberant yellow teeth and a matted, sooty forelock slicked down several times a day with fresh greasepaint. His unlovely appearance belied a startling aerodynamic elasticity exercised up the city's chimneys in vigorous defiance of a recent act of parliament outlawing the practice. Ezekiel Brown, known as Eazy, an appellation which described both his moral leanings and his philosophical outlook, had been spying for the curate for the best part of a year. His unorthodox method necessitated shimmying *down* the flue, instead of up it, in order better to snoop on his unsuspecting victims. It had recently become a family affair, the boy having introduced Kite to his mother Phyllis 'Flamingo Philly' Chang, third assistant dresser and onetime chorus girl. Philly had quite literally fallen on penurious times since her glory days as the best high kicker this side of the Strand until rumbling bursitis had forced her into early retirement after an unscheduled tumble into the orchestra pit. If this were not misfortune enough, her accident had coincided with her husband, a jobbing tailor, transforming their life's savings into a one-way ticket to Jermyn Street. Lithe, leggy and in the penumbral light of the wings rather pretty, Philly was all but illiterate, a quirk which allowed Kite's eloquent persuasions of surrender as a form of salvation to hit plausibly home. Her gymnastic agility invigorated him after the lethargy of his dreary wife, and he was content to provide a modest weekly stipend to avoid eviction from her damp rooms in St Clements so long as she accommodated him at his leisure. After all, he had exclaimed lightly, she had always opened her legendary legs for a living,

47

so why blither about it now? Conversation was best kept to a minimum, due in no small part to both mother and son's incomprehensible jargon, the tilt and sway of which exasperated him. She hadn't been hard to convince, the combination of charm and financial inducement had done the trick and then she was all too happy to 'Dab it up with him, handsome, if only for extra scran'. Within the last few weeks, however, she had grown exacting and fractious as his ardour had flourished along with his licence. Just last week she had yelled loud enough to wake the understudy "'Ere! I ain't no Judy for you to hit on the Nancy! Change yer tune or sling it, no matter how close to the big man you are!" Once deciphered, Kite was quick to contradict her; no rent money or the odd tap, which would she prefer? But he would have to watch her carefully. She had thus far afforded an outlet that he savoured, as well as endowing him with a backstage pass which enabled him to enjoy inconspicuously the comedy and crassness of the music hall in all its frenetic sensuality. More than once, he had been tickled to recognise famously aloof members of the faculty and even one or two punctilious clerics rabblerousing in the audience.

Her son now, there was an asset worth holding onto. Puck to Philly's Helena, he could put a girdle around the city's most august institutions in just under forty minutes. Eazy exhibited the kind of scant regard for life that the churchman considered highly profitable. The boy had assured his most 'olyful of 'olinesses than he'd do pretty much anything for a flatch, and that he had no qualms about secreting himself in the most sickening and noisome of hidey-holes so as to eavesdrop on Oxford's great and good. Bribery was a squalid draw on Kite's resources but a ha' penny now and then seemed worth it should such a course of action ever arise. There'd been nothing so far beyond the usual tawdry indiscretions but he had high hopes of his indefatigable acolyte.

What Kite could not know, even as he tightened his grip on Phil's shuddering shoulders, was that his wife and his servant were spending the evening in a most unforeseen manner, with the inimitable and muddleheaded Clara Pebble, weary and unsettled by her hospital vigil, choosing this moment to vent her spleen about the injustice of her employers' marriage. She admitted to no-one, nor would she ever, that she had spent many a miserable evening crouched outside their bedroom door, listening to the sounds of their enthusiastic congress even as she bit her nails so savagely that her fingers bled into her apron. She longed for the courage to ask Madam if she dared deny she enjoyed it with him, she'd heard her ringing cries that many times. Would it kill her to smile at him, instead of moping around the house like a bleedin' invalid? If she would just for once let her dress her, as she was paid to do, they might together bring some brightness into his life. Always so dull, why was Madam forever swathed in her drab, high-necked gowns? She warmed to her stride, wailing uncontrollably in the absence of the master, as accusations sparked scorching from her lips. "You don't deserve him! You with all your book learning and your beauty! He loves you so much and you never make him happy!" It was of course an outrageous and dischargeable transgression but Pauline, dignified and silent throughout the lengthy barrage, did not insist that Clara leave her service. Instead, she sent her straight to bed with a drop of brandy and a hot stone. She owed Linus' survival to the girl, and it was a debt she knew she could never repay.

When it became clear that the boy was out of danger, plans to dispatch him were reinstated and gathered pace. Somewhat paler, perhaps a little less humorous, Linus re-joined the household following a lengthy recuperation only to be told to pack his bags. By the time he was due to leave, both Pauline and Clara Pebble had reached an uneasy entente, if only to render their mutual melancholy a smidgen less lonely. The prompt arrival at the end of August of Greenwich Hospital School's official chaperone caused something of a stir at number 45. Dashing and exotic, the officer was a walking Velasquez, complete with a blade-thin black moustache and a double row of shining gold buttons; Linus was naturally thrilled to make his acquaintance. Despite Lieutenant Julian Domenico looking as if he had just disembarked from the Armada and claiming that yes, he was descended from the conquistadores on his mother's side, he had been born and raised in a British naval dynasty in Plymouth. He was just returned from visiting his sisters there and his mission was to accompany able seaman Hardcastle back to quarters, quick march and at the double, sir! While treachery twitched at Clara Pebble's heart, Kite treated him with disdain, declaring himself unable to see what all the fuss was about, but not before he had accused his wife of the most indelicate flirtation. The day the two set out for London was so unseasonably blustery and biting that Pauline wondered if she'd ever be warm again. She felt her brother's loss keenly; the void at the centre of her hollowed-out life swirled and dragged at her as remorselessly as a neap tide. Within a week of Linus' departure, the migrating birds all flew away and took what was left of the summer with them.

From "The Rape of Lucrece"
by William Shakespeare

What could he see but mightily he noted?
What did he note but strongly he desired?
What he beheld, on that he firmly doted,
And in his will his wilful eye he tired.
With more than admiration he admired
Her azure veins, her alabaster skin,
Her coral lips, her snow-white dimpled chin…

Chapter 4
Winter 1883, Kirtham:
Assault; Ambition Realised

Habitual as the chiming of the church clock, the noises nudging Pauline from her fitful dreams were soothingly familiar, if only to the initiated – thock, thock… plink – this same tintinnabulation had become a winter morning rite. Gideon East on his dawn patrol, breaking ice with cheery gusto, unvarying in his method: the sharp double tap with his wooden mallet on the icicles a-dangle on the stable roof, a soundless plummet and allegro tinkle as they splintered on the frosty ground. Soon they would melt away as if they had never been. Once, she would have wished to vanish with such brutally irrevocable efficiency. High on her hard wooden chair up in the nursery at Stonehaven, Pauline counted the sparrows as they circled in to roost in the eaves above the narrow window. Frowning at the sickly, custard-coloured walls she wondered if she had the courage to ask for the room to be redecorated, in perhaps a duck egg blue or apple green, something from nature. The baby was at peace in her arms and if the last sixth months had taught her anything, it was that snatched moments of slumber were as rare as fairy gold.

While her father's carpet softened the stone flags, the room was chill and the fire long extinguished but still she sat, deep in shadow, contemplating the path her life had taken. Dismissed for hours at a time to this cramped attic space by her increasingly truculent husband, her solitude had been uninterrupted apart from one momentous development, she was no longer alone; for the first time since her marriage, she knew the satisfaction of uncomplicated reciprocal love. Mother and daughter required no other company, they were each other's beating hearts; not since she parted from her brother had she felt so connected and so requisite. Now she had something to exist for and accordingly her life had taken on a new prospect: as Mrs Kite, the rector's obedient helpmeet amid the bright, hard glare of society, she felt like nothing more than a second-rate actress trotting out the same old tired lines but here in the quiet dark, hope for her newly incarnated future breathed in and out with fragile little lungs. She traced a gentle finger over two high points of colour in the baby's cheeks, joy or rage, as yet unpronounceable. The child was a barometer, affirming her mother's paradoxical realisations: she was endurance painfully rewarded, and she was freedom achieved in long captivity. Given the unconventional family's provenance, a muddled complexity would always threaten its equilibrium.

Here in the safety of exile, Pauline allowed herself to remember. Last autumn, with Linus not long removed, Kite had pulled like a savage dog on a short leash, hungry, aggressive and sulky with ennui. His promotion was slow in coming and he suffered the prevarication bitterly, imagining his superiors' perverse amusement as he proselytised from his stifling pulpit. His more intimate affairs were also provoking, his powers apparently waning. Philly had taken another lover, a soldier who had threatened to beat seven bells out of his thus far unidentified rival, see how he liked it. Eazy, far from unearthing a scandal, had himself been exposed, not to mention badly singed, by a corrupt alderman whose rapid disposal of a packet of comprising letters had resulted in the rallying of the Town Fire Brigade. The mutinous atmosphere in the house had been choking, mounting pressure at number 45 depressing them all, everyone's nerves were shredded and waiting for the inevitable detonation was almost insupportable. Finally, in mid-September there came news; the family would move into Kirtham Rectory in a twelvemonth. The next Harvest Festival service at St Mary the Virgin would be Kite's first undertaking as the Vicar of Akeman Benefice.

Thinking back now, how many times had she asked herself if she would change her destiny by just one whit? The most violent, traumatic and humiliating trial of her young life had unexpectedly thrown her a lifeline. Still, she should have been more vigilant when her husband suggested to Clara Pebble that she spend the weekend at her ageing mother's. Such spurious generosity signified a distress flare in the gathering fog, but his unruffled calm had lulled them both. No drifting flurries, no warning gusts had alerted her and the whirlwind, when it came, flattened all before it. Shifting in her seat, she drew a long and juddering breath. He had been jubilant; bursting in on her to announce that he had singlehandedly reaped a crop worthy of the season and demanding of her a contribution to his foison. Bewildered and uncomprehending, she was dangerously assailable. Since then, Pauline had erased, drafted and redrawn the ordeal so many times that all that was left was an incoherent outline like an over-exposed daguerreotype. Episodic flashes, streaks and sparks of faded images, along with tattered sensations of spasming agony, bone-deep smarting and a heaving, white-hot throb along her ribcage as she was bent over the edge of the hot cast-iron tub, her mouth knocking against the metal rim, the skin on her naked knees scraping the tiled floor as her husband energetically exercised his conjugal rights.

His exhilaration was short-lived and while she groped, drenched and spluttering, for her robe he thrust a towel at her, gesticulating towards her upper lip which had torn like jagged, red lightning. Kite had never beheld her so beautiful or so terrible; while her face was ivory pale, tendrils of wet-brick hair coiled like Medusa's snakes about her neck and in her eyes gleamed enigmatic flecks of dark green fire. To his horror, her freckled skin was efflorescing into mottled purplish blooms even as he watched, and a sensation he assumed must be shame rippled round the edges of his conscience. He left her spread-eagled in the bath's pinkish dregs, insisting that she exercise more care on the slippery floor, lest she cause herself a more serious injury.

The following Monday, Clara Pebble had clucked around her mistress with the carbolic, administering to the feverish patient with genuine concern. How on earth had she managed to crack her face open while taking a bath? Lordy, how was she to eat? Could she even talk? Would she like paper and one of her pencils instead, so Madam could communicate her wishes? Such a speedy onset, she hoped it wasn't the ague taking hold. Pauline would never know what made her decide to allow the maid finally into her confidence; she had simply arrived at a point in her wretched isolation that it was that or

55

self-destruction. With silent tears sliding into her pillow, she slowly raised her nightdress to reveal the angry inflammation beneath her chest, pointing wordlessly at the wedding portrait on the polished oak press. For a full half-minute Clara stood rigid, her mouth a perfect circle as she surveyed the injurious landscape of her mistress's ravaged body. Not long out of childhood herself, all she could think of was nursery fare to describe the indescribable; split greengages, over-ripe blackberries, strawberry jam splatters and smears of lemon curd. As the monumental misconception under which she had so slavishly laboured toppled to ruins, so too did her expression; it was as if every bone in her sharp little face had been extracted by some invisible hand. She sank to her knees beside the bed, sobbing "I'm sorry, I'm sorry, I'm so, so sorry," into the sheets, so wringing her hands and mewing and rolling her red-rimmed eyes that Pauline had sunk into fitful slumber convinced that the little maid had dissolved into Melpomene.

Winter that year had dragged its dismal pall over the city, clinging, fickle fog and icy wind-blown sleet obscuring the streets and sending people burrowing for home long before dusk. It had been mid-November when a slumped and dripping Dr Belshire had sounded the bell at number 45 St Giles, seeking shelter from the elements. Pauline bestowed upon her beloved godfather the same sincere and welcoming affection as in her childhood but there was no fooling the wily scientist. Something had profoundly affected the girl, her youthful, lustrous shine had been irreparably tarnished and he would swear he was looking at a woman of thirty years and more. Over tea and scones, he communicated Barnaby's best wishes and told her of his feisty colleague's reluctant surrender to a heavy head cold some days ago. Already, he chuckled; the lawyer had defended two tricky cases from his bed in strict contravention of medical instructions. It was almost like old times and Pauline hoped her flimsy façade might hold until the final moments of his visit. Instead, turning abruptly on the sofa to face her, he had asked, quietly, politely and penetratingly, how long she had been in her present condition and was she in any pain? Even he could not mistake her convulsing tears for those of joy, but still she had not shared the whole truth with him. As Belshire was taking his leave, the man of the house had arrived home and received cordially his felicitations, quoting from Ephesians 6:4 even as he closed the door firmly behind the departing doctor.

A dazzling December had brought better times. When the curate set out on a long overdue expedition to the Midlands to share the happy news with his extended family, it was understood that his wife should not accompany him and when worsening weather forced an extension of his stay over the Christmas season Pauline felt that she had received the best gift of all. Tipsy with emancipation, she and a playful Clara Pebble festooned the house with fragrant holly and baked marzipan bells before stoking all the fires and luxuriating in front of a pine-scented blaze. The two leaned together in adversity and while they would never be friends, their respective positions discouraged it, Clara was proudly watchful, fetching balm for Madam's swollen ankles and rubbing her back when she felt queasy. After months of suffocation, both were intoxicated by the fresh air. They were like school children at the clang of the Friday bell, strolling through the snowy city and beside the frozen Cherwell, bird watching, berry-gathering and swapping stories about Linus.

While a brief shadow flitted over the holiday in the form of a letter from Greenwich with news of her brother's decision to remain at school with his friends for the festivities, Christmas Day dawned happy and hopeful. Clara accompanied her mother and her mistress in the singing carols at church before heading back for lunch as the light faded and while the old lady dozed, they found themselves comparing their separate futures. The maid had already been apprised by Kite that her frankly pitiful services were no longer required once they'd relocated, and she already looked forward to seeking work in a teashop in town when the time was right. As she lay merrily down to sleep that night, she sifted through the keepsakes of this her most memorable day: if she had to choose but one, it would be how she had squirmed fit to burst to hear Madam express her delight in her 'Very pretty smile', assuring her that it quite transformed her countenance. Well, honestly, who'd have thought it?

The women's gentle accommodation had proved a boon during Pauline's uncomfortable pregnancy. All through the burgeoning spring, Clara was vigilant and attentive, keeping her warm, cooling her down, soothing or stimulating without having to be asked or rewarded; Pauline knew it was a kind of penance, but she was grateful, nonetheless. Kite had remained greedy for her but uncharacteristically discreet, leaving no outward traces on her stretching skin but making his demands with a degree of force that might not be refused. As her time drew near, Pauline felt intermittently fearful and then excited by the change that was coming. These things never went according to plan Dr Belshire had promised her, and so it came to pass. One warm, drizzly June evening, Clara Pebble had astonished her once again by efficiently delivering a daughter with the minimum of fuss and a professionalism beyond her years. When a faintly steaming Dr Manley finally wheezed up the stairs, he was forced to admit that the girl indeed exhibited some small measure of merit. Never mind how tidy the birth had been, the strangely silent nursling emerged the very picture of pain with a cleft lip and a fire-red halo of hair as with her first breath she seared into her mother's heart the question: could she love Kite's child? The answer arrived simultaneously with the aghast father; with this little girl, she would lay the foundations of her own stone circle, unbreakable. She shuddered as she recalled how Kite had stared down at their offspring, horrified, bitterly disappointed, and then monumentally enraged. He had charged her viciously with infidelity, vehemently denying the baby's paternity, listing the effects of syphilis in new-borns. There and then their brittle marriage had fatally fractured like one of East's icicles. Kite officiated at the christening merely to keep up appearances and made no demur at the name Brianna, which Pauline had chosen in memory of her mother and its connotations of indomitability. Confinement, endorsed by medical opinion and enforced by her husband, was extended indefinitely and mother and child were from then on to all intents and purposes incarcerated within the boundaries of number 45, whereupon time promptly began to lose its meaning. The curate once or twice had feigned distress to his parish, letting it be known that his wife had been afflicted by a post-natal malaise which was slow to lift but in truth he grew uneasy in the presence of his family and preferred to stay away. His customary confidence had faded along with Pauline's recent bruises and become something else entirely; he was outnumbered. Mark, you, the brat disturbed him from the start, so uncannily mute, emitting no more than a low moan to signify agitation. He could swear that she snarled at him, twisting her scarred mouth in scorn and fixing him with eyes that reminded him of thick moss on a tombstone. Those early days as a father growled like a roving storm, a rallying disorderly darkness which the sun could never penetrate. For a few months he exercised a dreary dissimulation in front of visiting doctors but he quickly lost interest. It suited him well that in Kirtham rumours were already rife; a mad wife, a maimed baby, a cursed family arriving to seek the Lord's redemption. The poor, handsome rector was a living saint, who would blame him if he were to send away both mother and child, the one to the asylum and the other for adoption by the nuns?

Suddenly, Pauline was conscious of her daughter stretching against her shoulder. Planting a soft kiss on the tawny fuzz of her crown, she swallowed her rising dread and forced herself to remember. Her beloved Oxford had been immortalised in the mournful strains of Mozart's Requiem drifting through the open doors of Christchurch Cathedral as she waved Clara Pebble off and in the direction of the High Street towards her new employer. The move to Kirtham had been lonely and fraught but here they were still together, mother and child. She kept reminding herself that while it would never be home, there was much to appreciate about Stonehaven and its rural situation. The house, very much her husband's domain, was architecturally splendid but she viewed it simply as a hollow void that stubbornly took against filling. There were endless ringing acres of polished floors and yawning fireplaces, huge gaping gilt mirrors and drooping swathes of heavy drapery. She preferred to be outside, exploring the extensive greenery beyond the formal gardens, the prehistoric ginkgo tree had produced in her such a wild pang for her mother that only armfuls of wild flowers from the grasslands behind the servants' quarters could begin to form a suitable distraction. Most of all she was enchanted by the two thick-set apple trees freighted with dusky fruit outside the kitchen window, for all the world like a dancing couple paused forever mid-waltz. She had set up her paints and easel there and was at times almost happy, establishing a habit of painting in the pink light of dawn. Her characteristic stillness had allowed her to enjoy the various attentions of a cautious vixen sniffing the windfalls, a hedgehog on a snuffling crusade across the dewy lawn and even a drowsy muntjac, which had skipped out from the thick shrubbery at the back wall and approached her so nearly that she could feel its hot breath on her hand. Despite a talkative family of jackdaws resident in the branches, hers remained a largely friendless existence and Kite had made sure that his new flock understood her condition; acutely photosensitive, melancholic, she was better suited to confinement for her own protection. Her highly suspicious godfathers had been summarily turned away from number 45 just before the Kites had quit the house. Mr Barnaby remained perplexed in the extreme following his friend's report. "Skittish anxiety about imminent motherhood I can comprehend, even applaud so instinctive does it seem but the way you describe it, our poor, dear girl is now a victim of…"

"Fear," concluded a solemn Dr Belshire.

And so, in a way, she was. With motherhood had come trepidation even as resignation had hardened into resistance. Her own status as a victim had been like slow drowning but now, she was responsible for another living creature and granted the licence that accompanies fierce guardianship. Most lonely women feared the grip of madness pulling them under, she had read enough of the Bronte sisters' work to recognise that. But negotiating these fickle currents between outrage and defiance on one bank of the swirling river, subservience and obscurity on the other was nigh on impossible. While the diagnosis of this solely female affliction remained the exclusive reserve of the opposite sex, what chance did she have of staying afloat? Only now did she realise that marriage, the destination of so many of her kind, was not the life raft she had artlessly presumed it to be, and the waters were rising.

Christmas rolled inexorably around again, their first at Kirtham but how different this would be from last year's blissful hiatus. By seven this evening, the peaceful house would be pulsing with guests, and she would assume the role of wife again, like a chrysalis in reverse. Six-month-old Brianna must remain in the nursery with one of the housemaids, she was too young and unpredictable to be part of the celebrations according to her husband but Pauline knew he was mordantly ashamed of her. He was putting his considerable energies into establishing himself as a martyr, a husband and father who could not go far enough to ensure the wellbeing of his flawed family and who had let it be widely known that he was seeking therapies and treatments if recommendations could be made. Was there ever a more blatant appeal for confederacy? And they had flocked to him, as he knew they would, eager to be part of the entourage of a clerical hero endorsed not only by the Dashwood family of Kirtham Park but by the bishop himself. She pictured his disciples seated around the dining table in a grovelling parody of Da Vinci's Last Supper. Publican Joshua Smithers from the Oxford Arms, wall-eyed but tender-hearted, with abroad smile like a spade in a turnip; his near neighbours the widowed sisters Jemima and Isobel Chance, both obese and immobile apart from tiny black eyes like currants pushed too far into wet dough; the hearty Boxers, Gabriel and Andrew, proud breeders of prize-winning Tamworths, a generous dusting of hayseed mottling their breeze-blown beards; the sanctimonious Ipplepens, Edwin and his cadaverous wife Amelia, the former a successful international tea merchant with puritan sensibilities and a capitalist's bank balance. The Bits from the dairy, Publius Bit every inch the proud paterfamilias, corpulent and effusive with a straining, striped waistcoat and fat white eyebrows wriggling like demented caterpillars across his florid brow. His wife Esmeralda was a startlingly diminutive, bird-like creature of whom it was scarcely to be credited that she had birthed no fewer than eight children: four graceless daughters, the ornately named Fuchsia, Magnolia, Forsythia and Wisteria all of whom were the spit of their father. The sons favoured their mother and had to be accommodated on sofas long before the women due to weak lungs and frail bones. Mrs Bit had called a moratorium at boy number four with the result that her husband was denied a full complement of evangelists; Matthew, Mark, Luke and Albert, the last named for the queen's consort as mark of respect, nonetheless limped towards a reluctant eligibility among the village's unmarried girls. And then Pauline's favourite, the kind-eyed local apothecary Mr Ishir Choudhry, recently disembarked from Madras via Tilbury with nothing but his copious credentials and an encyclopaedic knowledge of botanical medicines. He had arrived bearing gifts of colourful spices, shot-silk napkins and restorative, highly perfumed stews that Kite regarded with barely concealed scepticism. All of them were intrigued by the wraithlike figure of the rector's wife, so beautiful and so, so sad. What in heaven's name was to be done?

Down in the pantry the cook-cum-housekeeper was painstakingly counting out chestnuts and wondering where the Missus might have hidden herself now. Florrie Root knew a wrong 'un when she saw one and congratulated herself on being able to spot a charlatan, whether it was trussed up in a dog collar or not. She had come to Stonehaven nearly thirty years ago as a slender scullery maid and grown exponentially in direct proportion to her cheerful years of service. Almost completely spherical, she resembled a vast blancmange endowed with the daintiest of hands and feet. Friendly brown eyes peeked out from under prematurely white hair, piled high like a rampant, frothy spume of meringue. Every day she donned the same conker-brown bombazine housecoat but this winter she had surreptitiously treated herself to a pair of angora mittens which she would whip off as soon as anyone approached the kitchen. Given to prolific and animated soliloquy, and with a gift for hyperbole, her voice was high and reedy like a querulous child. Very, very few people realised that she was missing the third finger of her left hand, an injury apparently sustained while rescuing her beloved Sealyham terrier from the jaws of death, or at least those of a tetchy Irish wolfhound. Nobody but nobody knew the real and equally savage story which involved her addle-brained husband, a stevedore at Liverpool docks, lunging drunkenly for her wedding ring to pay for one last tot of rum. Up to then a devout Methodist, she now found herself immovably stalled on the first of the four alls having met the new rector, whose methods of persuasion struck her as uncannily similar to those of her erstwhile spouse. The unflagging Mrs Root only enjoyed sufficient leisure time to nurture one genuine friendship and that was with an ageing librarian in Leamington Spa, to whom she sent weekly bulletins in the thrilling style of her favourite author, Mr Collins. She had read The Woman in White forty-seven times since its publication. When first she had set eyes on Mrs Kite, she had been not just star-struck but psychologically astute; despite her pale attire, this was no Anne Catherick, this, as she lived and breathed, was Laura Fairlie, in her own pantry, fancy that! The woman was skin and bone, gaunt as halibut bones. And agoraphobic too, it seemed, never venturing further than the church next door and even then, muffled up to the eyebrows. Tch, tch, that husband of hers made no attempt to fatten her up but then handsome is as handsome does, she supposed. To Pauline's mind, she was a formidable guardian angel wielding a ladle: Mrs R's patented philosophy? A soup for every occasion. When they had first arrived, mother and baby wan and drooping in the doorway, she had sized them up with her head cocked on one side and lost no time in whipping up a mulligatawny, quick you like. Her kindness was instinctive, her generosity borne of a fullness of heart that asked nothing in return. Soon after their arrival, having heard the Missus talk so affectionately about one Miss Pebble, she had managed to winkle out recent tidings of her from the miller who supplied flour and yeast to both the Rectory and Miss Muldoon's Muffins and More in Blue Boar Street, Clara's place of work. Well now, that had been a very pretty day and Missus had hugged the cook so winningly that she had vowed to keep the lines of communication open, even if it meant baking on a Sunday.

The scent of icing sugar sifted into the nursery seconds ahead of the rustle and clip, clip and rustle which heralded the arrival of the housekeeper and her faithful Wilkie along the tiled passageway. "And there she is!" fluted Mrs Root, sweeping Brianna out of Pauline's arms and nestling her against her colossal bosom. "Would you look at her, the wee mite? Why, I could eat her little face off!" and with that the insatiable domestic bustled away with the baby, cooing about silver garlands, mulled wine and gingerbread. Much to Pauline's tacit amusement, the dignified old dog had disliked her husband on sight and took every opportunity to harass him. A good day was when he managed to purloin something of the Reverend's to chew, the shredding of silk handkerchiefs constituted a distinction, an acme achieved only once thus far and paid for with a sharp kick in the flank. She could hear Mrs Root debating with herself genially between bacon and barley broth or spiced pumpkin velouté for the guests tonight and as she made her way down to the kitchen, redolent with the festive scents of mincemeat and oranges, Pauline sent up the first of many silent prayers for a peaceful Christmas.

From "A Vindication of the Rights of Woman"
by Mary Wollstonecraft

"My own sex, I hope, will excuse me, if I treat them like rational creatures, instead of flattering their fascinating graces, and viewing them as if they were in a state of perpetual childhood, unable to stand alone. I earnestly wish to point out in what true dignity and human happiness consists – I wish to persuade women to endeavour to acquire strength, both of mind and body, and to convince them that the soft phrases, susceptibility of heart, delicacy of sentiment, and refinement of taste, are almost synonymous with epithets of weakness, and that those beings who are only the objects of pity and that kind of love, which has been termed its sister, will soon become objects of contempt."

Chapter 5
Summer 1885, Kirtham:
The Winds of Change

The outgoing rector had bequeathed to his successor a manservant whom he took venial pride in describing as proof of God's benign presence on earth, so complete was his transformation following a life of senseless and brutish violence. His conversion, the churchman vaunted, had boosted attendance at St Mary's threefold, villagers flocking to witness not only the former soldier's singular religious zeal but to listen to his operatic baritone now deployed to ecstatic effect in the choir stalls. Originally from Welsh valley mining stock Osian Jones had fled the family business for the Fusiliers as soon as he could wield a pen convincingly enough to mark the joining papers. Configured like an inverted pyramid, squat, bull-necked and bullet-bald despite a bristling, Colman's-coloured moustache, his prominent nose had been spectacularly broken following a misjudged encounter at too close quarters with a spiked Russian helmet in the Crimea. Alas, the same ponderous maladroitness had dogged his passage through the ranks while the subtle soubriquet Juggernaut Jones went some way to hint at his military tactics.

In late middle age, the ill-starred Corporal had been employed at Stonehaven in the spirit of philanthropic rehabilitation following a dishonourable discharge, the reason for which had been lost, perhaps felicitously, to time. The man had nothing to recommend him but a reputation as a champion presser of collars and a lugubriously obsequious air, second nature after decades of incontestable commands. A slave to duty, Jones silently patrolled the corridors of the Rectory, stopping only to salute his new employer with a click of his heels and a musical "Rev-er-rend Sah!" as he snapped, as far as he was rheumatically able, to attention. He secreted about his person at all times a small silver crucifix, to guard against assault from the ungodly. Despite what was charitably classified as a messianic glint in his pugnacious eye, Jones was more than a little selective in his theological study. Pressed by his employer, he had plodded laboriously up to the moment where Eve had offered a bite of her apple, whereupon he had shrugged his gargantuan shoulders and read no further, declaring himself of the opinion that all women were temptresses and harlots, let that be an end to it. Confidentially, he considered Mrs Kite a veritable wisp of a hussy, the most insidious kind, and as for the child, she was surely sent by the devil himself. Thus far, his duties as valeting butler had not proved too onerous but his morbid mistrust of unarmed and peaceable society affected his public announcement of callers to the point of debilitation. In particular, that witch doctor Choudhry was no better than he should be, God knew. He'd met his sort in Afghanistan, had he not? A heathen born, let him try to deny it. Neither the finer points of geography, nor a cheery wave from the back pews of St Mary's of a Sunday could budge this notion once it had lodged itself in Jones' somewhat battered cranium. No, the foreigner was up to something, for sure. Jones would petition the Lord for guidance, yes, that was the way.

The humanitarian apothecary was nothing if not tenacious, bearing on this fine early summer's day, and precisely, in this order his compliments, a variety of fruit tisanes and a recommendation for the treatment of the downcast Mrs Kite. His first interview was with the patient herself, with whom he shared such tender and solicitous concerns touching his dear wife, en route from India as they spoke, that Pauline was almost moved to tears, a reaction which went some way to confirm his informal diagnosis of lingering post-partum melancholia. Conversing later with the rector, Choudhry recounted how, after much consideration, his medical acquaintances had suggested that the Radcliffe Infirmary might be at liberty to supply not just a qualified caregiver but one of its star practitioners. The situation was not without its delicacy, Nurse Budden being temporarily indisposed by a raft of deep and unsightly scratches on her face and neck, the parting gift of a dying lunatic by the bedside of whom, it was rumoured, she had sat for three consecutive days and nights, holding her down and whispering consolations while the woman bucked and heaved her way into eternal darkness. He'd soon been apprised of the truth of this sensitive case, which concerned a downtrodden seamstress, apprehended attempting to bury a warm bundle in a drainage ditch off the Iffley Road. Horrified witnesses reported a needle swinging from her bloodied lips, and further investigation had revealed a neat, cross-stitched seam across her baby's mouth. Choudhry, while new to the village, was a shrewd and observant judge of character; he was confident he

70

had the measure of his vicar and that he responded best to flattery, not facts. At the Infirmary, the professors and surgeons were just now united in the decision to grant the young professional in question a substantial leave of six months absence, not just for her own recuperation but to relieve the patients of their distress on seeing their favourite thus maimed. A pleasing symmetry, was it not Mr Kite, the nurse and her charge, healing together? For such two such charming women cannot surely be ailing for long, in this bucolic setting and with God's blessing, both might recover themselves, no? In the face of the chemist's smiling benevolence, there was little Kite could do but agree to a trial period. Who knew, perhaps a woman thus disfigured might be a little freer with her favours? What Jones would do with another female in the house wasn't worth thinking about but at least the village would be forced to admire their rector's attentive ministrations.

Two years to the day that Brianna was born, Nurse Elinor Budden blew in to Kirtham. Gideon East, groundsman and general factotum, had grumbled all the way to Oxford, rumbling along in the fly and blueing the air with fantastical curses but by the time they turned the corner back into the village, he was smitten, he admitted it. He had been advised about her lacerations and expected at least a veil but in this he underestimated his passenger. Though severe, she wore her injuries with such unselfconscious lightness, more a noble kind of pride, that after an unmanly gawp and a couple of hard swallows, he soon forgot them. She had hoisted herself up into the vehicle as if it were a hearthside rocking chair but not before hefting her modest trunk on board with her own strong, brown arms. Tiny silver shells glinted in her ears and when she shook his skinny hand vigorously and expressed a friendly greeting, he knew that he had never met anyone like her. The priceless looks that had been thrown their way as they bowled along the track, her shining, chestnut hair loose and tumbling wild in the breeze, cheeks rosy with sunshine and generous mouth defaulting to a wide grin. Nurse Budden was a force of nature, at the altar of which she bent the knee. Trim and ruddy, clad in a short shoulder cape, clean-coloured like a heathery ice-capped sea, her medical vocation went far beyond a sling and a cold compress. She had an instinct for empathy and a faith in organic healing over superfluous pharmaceuticals. As she settled in beside him, East had detected beneath her starched linen smell something trailing in the air like incense or moss, maybe peat, something of the earth. She's a hardy 'un, that maid, he thought to himself, here's hoping she can cure the lot of them.

Barrelling up Stonehaven's looping drive, her first assessment was not a favourable one and she tried to suppress the evocation of the gloomy asylum in which she had completed her training. There too were rows of windows compounding a contrary sense of imprisonment. She had anticipated warm, sunny Cotswold stone, sheets snapping on a line in the back garden and the sounds of an al fresco family at play but was it just her or did a haughty aloofness hang about the place? The Rectory was coolly majestic, studded with porches and terraces, approached by a stately avenue and flanked by manicured lawns. That was it, she realised as they drew up to the house, everything was very much in its place here. Which was why her eye was drawn to a pale flapping shape high at an open window under the roof. Squinting, she tried to make it out; a servant perhaps, signalling furiously but a friendly greeting or a hurried warning? Maybe the house was haunted? She grinned broadly and waved up at the figure, which promptly vanished.

Not for the likes of her the smartly varnished teak front door which led, she assumed, into the main vestibule. She just had time to raise her eyebrows at a grotesque brass knocker in the form of a satyr's face so contorted and leering that it made her want to cross herself before she was whisked round to the narrow servants' entrance beyond a muddy rectangular courtyard much decorated with horse manure. Wedged in the doorway a giantess brandishing a wooden spoon was disputing the price of two scrawny rabbits with a grimy poacher who was rapidly losing ground. Smartly negotiating a discount for both, the awesome female then spat in her hand to seal the deal, promised to keep quiet when the rozzers called and delivered a fruity wink in the nurse's direction. Mrs Root, once comfortably settled with a cup of tea back in her airy kitchen, introduced herself properly and before a syllable could be exchanged launched into a protracted monologue in explanation of the newcomer's – "I'll call you Elinor, if I may, I may, mayn't I?" – facial injuries which endured for at least three pieces of more than palatable lemon cake.

"Feral cat then, was it? Happens all the time. Me, I prefer dogs, you know where you are with dogs, right Wilkie?" She finally drew breath, pausing to pat the head of an ageing terrier with its head on her lap which had regarded her throughout with patient adoration. Nurse Budden was so delighted to have made a friend that she forgot her misgivings instantly and the two proceeded to cement their bond over the Lord's intention regarding cold soup. It seemed that 'Vicious-wise' had been ordered for dinner that very evening and Mrs

Root was flummoxed, she didn't mind telling her. Mutual laughter ensued, heads thrown back and crumbs spraying everywhere, much to Willkie's gratification. And what of her patient, what was she like? At once the cook assumed a grave expression and huffed in deep frustration, speaking in hushed, dramatic tones. She was sure she couldn't say exactly, ghostly and fading, most of her time spent at the top of the house in that spooky nursery with that sorry little babe, her pride and joy, mind you, she lived for that little darling... At which point, there materialised noiselessly in the doorway a woman clad all in white, with a perplexed look in her turbulent, sea-green eyes. She was shaking her finely shaped head and agitating with low, lyrical hesitation about whether she had done right to open the upper casement, letting a trapped moth out into the summer air. She might have scooped it into a dark cupboard and closed the doors instead for its own safety, what did they think, please?

Nurse Budden was starting to formulate her reply when an eccentrically proportioned creature who was surely embarking a second career after a stint in the circus marched in and ordered her to come along 'er him, immediately thereafter avoiding all possible association with her, both verbal and physical, with ludicrous ingenuity. All attempts to draw him into conversation were histrionically ignored and before long, she found herself in Rector Kite's richly furnished study with its views across the parterre to the wooded perimeter. The niceties, blunt and brief, being over, she was instructed imperiously in her duties and realised that she was there on sufferance. She must keep to her room at the top of the servants' stairs whenever society called; Mrs Kite was to remain shrouded at all times when in public view; the child was strictly not to be indulged. She nearly bobbed a curtsey until she remembered who she was. He never once sought her medical opinion and was hard-pressed to conceal what looked like disappointment despite his gaze ranging over her person in what she considered a most suggestive manner. His eyes were incontrovertibly arresting but she had still come away with an impression of leaden and lifeless ashes. A cold fish but for his hot blood, she had met his kind before and was astonished that a career in the church suited him. His wife, though, there she found herself intrigued. This case would take all her diplomacy, tact and intuition. The woman was woefully deficient in vitamin D and iron, malnourished and in a state of some anxiety. Highly articulate but almost mute with anxiety, her smile was like lit tinder after the nurse reassured her, she would have freed the creature too. And that radiant russet hair! So tightly bound and bundled out of sight even in the utter seclusion of her own room. Tomorrow's aim would be to compromise on a loose plait down her back, relax her scalp and ease her temples a bit. Nurse Budden did not share Mr Kite's verdict of light sensitivity; his wife's delicate skin was freckled and fair but nowhere near to the point of albinism, as her long, dark lashes confirmed. The sorry toddler was in a less than robust state of health, but she was in no position to look after herself. Sunshine and exercise, that was the initial prescription on meeting her charges, and what better place than here to affect the change?

The next morning Pauline woke to a beaker of ox-eye daisies nodding cheerfully next to her bed. A dawn-fresh breeze was rolling unexpectedly through the Rectory as Nurse Budden went round the house flinging wide the windows.

When the two had breakfasted, she asked Mrs Kite to accompany her on a turn about the garden, strapping Brianna to her back with all the skill and confidence of a hunting Eskimo. By then, the atmosphere in the entertaining rooms was thick with the cloying scent of cut flowers. Wilting in the rising heat, their water already tinted green with slime, bloated chrysanthemums shed petals like bloody tears while sweating orange lilies retched pollen onto polished wood, dusting the mahogany with bright poison rings. As suspected, outside was a carefully controlled massacre, great piles of rejected blooms lay in a freakish pyre behind the stables; it seemed like every growing thing within sight had been hacked, pruned, severed and spliced. Pauline slowed at the end of the path and pointed to the church beyond the fence: the extent of her freedoms was curtailed here, that was clear. Under the black wooden lych-gate one stubborn and neglected spear of dog rose had encroached, sprawling across the paving, brilliant white like a splash of gloss paint against the stone. Settling a gurgling Brianna down on the warm grass amid a pair of pirouetting red admirals, Elinor did two things. First, she very casually mooted the idea of a walk beyond the walls of the Rectory, perhaps tomorrow, while the weather held and the rector was away opening a fete in the next village. Then she recounted a story from her childhood, explaining how it had afforded her some small sense of her own identity. Her parents had nicknamed her Nora; well, she was having none of it, not even at six years old. She had reasoned with them thus: she was neither a dog chewing a stick nor a pair of dentures, thanks all the same. Pa and Mam had been tickled and kept giggling? "Neither, nor! Neither, nor!" said delightedly to each other. And 'Nor' had stuck, and it still made her smile because she found it for herself, and would Pauline mind if she called her by her first name, too, Mrs Kite being something of a mouthful?

And so it was that Kite's heavily veiled and voiceless wife was coaxed beyond the borders of her own existence. As the two took turns to hold Brianna's sticky hand, streaks of honeysuckle smouldered in the untamed hedgerows and hot, white dust swirled about their ankles, striping the child's cheeks like a little warrior ready for the fray. Beyond the dairy and down the unpaved track, they threaded their way past the quarry towards the river. Pausing for breath in the stacked shade of freshly excavated blocks of limestone, Nor initiated a debate about mining the land for its treasure. She was of the opinion that digging deep deserved some kind of reward but had to admit defeat in the face of Pauline's quiet consideration that the earth's dilated wounds made for a poor human legacy. The further they roamed, the more at ease the latter seemed to grow and when they finally settled under a spreading willow tree, she drew off her light glove and unbuttoned her cuff unthinkingly, trailing her fingers in the cool stream. Instantly, a smutch of dark, mottled dabs along the underside of her wrist lit up in the water. Nor made no acknowledgement, continuing to chuck the toddler under the chin as she dangled her little legs in a muddy tributary. Self-harm was not unusual in cases such as these but surprising in one so devoted to the welfare of her infant. "I shall remember these clawings long after they've faded," she said, fixing her dark eyes on Pauline's face. "But I shall strive hard to erase the influence they wield upon the balance of my mind. They were inflicted on me, but they do not define me. They will heal as I will. And so will you." Not another word was spoken and neither did it need to be. The afternoon assumed a miasmic quality, suspended and inviolable. At length, Brianna started to whimper as finally the shadows lengthened and they could delay no longer the return to Stonehaven and a different kind of silence.

Over the next three weeks, the pale summer skies burned with possibilities as Nor practised her therapy, sharing with her patient anecdotes from her past, depicting with such evocative yearning images of her hometown that Pauline felt as if she'd been taken on a personal tour. "Colmer's Hill," the canny nurse continued. "That's always when I know I'm nearly back where I belong; just outside of Bridport, a steep slope that's like a child's doodle, on the very top of which there waves a tuft of hardy pines. It's a hike up a sheep's track but when you're up there you are afforded the best view of the Dorset countryside for miles around! In winter it looks just like clotted cream on a bowl of spinach." She'd lived in Lyme Regis all her life, in a cottage up on Silver Street with her twin sisters. She was lucky and she knew it. Hers was a tight-knit town, crooked in the strong arm of the distinctive pier and watched over by the black cliffs of the bluff. She had spent her childhood wandering its sand and shingle beach and navigating the short, sharp slopes linking its twisted little lanes. She'd always been a quiet one, studious and fascinated by the natural world. Once, noticing only at bedtime that his eldest daughter was no longer where she should be, Pa Budden had fog-horned across the beach, crunching along the razor clams with a gaggle of anxious neighbours, only to be treated to a colourful piece of her ten-year-old mind for scaring off the barnacles that she swore were just inching out of their shells. Theirs were the best sunsets on the south coast, a glowing tamarind sky washing the bay with light, gilding the cliffs across from the harbour for a few seconds before tipping into the sea like a mess of melted caramel. "And the morning mist!" Nor braided Pauline's hair with a vigour born of reminiscent pride. "So thick that you can't see Charmouth until it peels back from the cliffs as if it were a lady's woollen stocking!" Sure enough, just as she had hoped, it wasn't long until a parallel tale evoking Oxford, Patch and Birdie was forthcoming, and it was by this circuitous route that the determined Nor first learned about Linus and his banishment to Greenwich.

Pauline would remember the precise hour of the very day that she received first-hand news of her brother after nearly three long years. Kite had strictly forbidden their communication, deeming it detrimental to her convalescence to pander to distractions of such an emotionally draining kind and she had often wondered with dismay if Linus had been notified of the move to Stonehaven. Shortly after ten in the morning on the fourteenth of August, Nor had found her stationed at her easel and pressed into her pocket a letter, addressed to Nurse Elinor Budden of The Radcliffe Infirmary care of the Rectory, Kirtham. She had wept happy tears at its contents and flown immediately to her room to pen a reply. This then was their second confidence but it would be nowhere near their last. The missive had brought immediate benefits to the health of the patient, as her nurse had suspected it must; Pauline grew sunny along with the weather and accompanied Nor and Brianna to church that Sunday with a thankful heart. Preparing for luncheon on their return, the nurse was in contemplative mood following a particularly wearisome sermon, sharing her meditations surrounding such various everyday apparatus as belts and braces, corsets and stays. It seemed, did it not, that men were habitually held up and supported but women constrained and kept in? "Blow me down, there's summat in that, for sure," muttered an enraptured Mrs Root, head aslant and buttery hands on hips.

Mr Choudhry could not have foreseen how his hopes for what he had termed a 'symmetry' between the two would develop. Synchronicity informed their association from the start, and each felt themselves roundly improved by the other in a most edifying fashion. Pauline, having explained the literary genesis of her name, was charmed to learn of her nurse's heroine, the entrepreneurial Eleanor Coade, after whom she had been christened by her grandfather, a master stonemason in her employ. Similarly, when a mortified Nor admitted that she had come by the chip in her front tooth leaping off the Cobb in a peevish adolescent rage, the other pondered if such a distinctive and rather charming blemish was the price to pay for not being caught by a gentleman, and wished they could consult Miss Austen on the matter. As the nurse patiently gained her trust, the straps and buckles on Pauline's strait jacketed life were loosened one by one until she found herself shuffling off the yoke of her invalid status like an itinerant hermit crab, vitality and purpose enriching her blood like wine. There were very few secrets she did not feel safe to disclose, not least the details surrounding Brianna's conception and the extent of the rector's neglect, most of which Nor had already divined. For so long she had lived without hope, with just perilous unpredictability and a ticking, frustrated rage for close company. Rendering, however incrementally, revelatory confidences into someone else's consciousness permitted Pauline to reclaim fragments of herself and begin the reassembly of her own self-portrait. Theirs was a mutually beneficial connection; for now, it masqueraded as a parlour game played in simple rhetoric but they knew that beneath the spoken words surged limitless prospects. In society, both were conscripted to the nameless and indeterminate ranks of 'She' and 'Her', anonymous like a floor of forest ferns in the dark. Only by allowing each other to stretch into the half-forgotten dimensions of 'I' or 'Me' could they begin a careful conjugation of the plural 'We', after which their clandestine friendship, open to the wind like a cross-pollinating field of poppies, blossomed into something that neither could yet define.

By summer's end, Mrs Kite and her confidante had become familiar fixtures in Kirtham, their dignified perambulations, always conducted in the befitting attire, arousing admiring comment and genuine esteem. Their furthest excursions, beyond the twitching curtains of the gentry, always seemed to coincide with Kite's more frequent absences which, given recent pressing invitations to administer his bespoke brand of spiritual guidance to a very charming widow out near Banbury, called for a fresh pair of watchful eyes, or in this case two. In the Chance house, the sedentary sisters, installed by the netting across their mullioned windows overlooking the Green were only too thrilled to report back to their dear rector, despite finding themselves infuriated, unable to manufacture the smallest discrepancy regarding the propriety of the young women. Indeed, Kite found himself fatigued by their gushing intelligence and largely dispassionate regarding his wife's activities. So far removed from his own advancement, her life remained of little interest to him, but he was keen to regain absolute control, something "that woman" had denied him of late; yes, he very much looked forward to her leaving his service straight after Christmas as per the original agreement. He agreed that she had put some flesh on his wife's waiflike bones, and he admitted privately that the new arrangement of the patient's hair was most stimulating in a schoolgirlish way but the nurse had rocked the equilibrium of his authority and she couldn't go soon enough. Lately, he had been forced to threaten East with the loss of his position on discovering that his infatuated groundsman had been supplying her with a horse to ride at her whim through the park and if he wasn't mistaken even old Jones appeared to be softening after she had supplied him with a tub of stinking liniment for his aching bones. No discernment these servant types – he'd have to tighten up the rules of his household forthwith.

Pauline did not allow herself to contemplate Nor's removal; life without her seemed unthinkable. Towards the middle of September, she took a final gamble, confiding her crippling fears concerning her beloved daughter. Never were the remarks or injuries to be found on the child but she was beginning to retreat within herself, purple swatches sat under her eyes, and she seemed jumpy as a cat. She had finally asked what Kite insisted could not be spoken of. Was the facial disfigurement permanent? Would Brianna never talk? Nor had sat across from Pauline at the scrubbed pine kitchen table and uttered words of such grave conviction that she was at once consoled. Brianna's condition was rare but, in many cases, speech had been facilitated and even perfected in the very young. Why, weren't her own dear sisters, Harriet and Flora, employed in a local church school for disadvantaged children and working with just this kind of infirmity among the poor denizens of Dorset?

As autumn freshened and a scattering of rust rimed the trees, the two discussed nothing so much as the youngster, stopping short of naming her the subconscious symbol of their own prospects. After nigh on four months spent almost entirely in each other's company, there bloomed a silent sympathy between them, powerfully nourished by the same dreams and prayers. There was nothing impulsive or erratic, nothing speculative or obscure in either heart, for surely ecstasy and exhilaration have their counterparts in moments of uncertainty or pause. Instead, the two shared a profound accommodation of perfect harmony. One afternoon, as the sun slipped behind the church spire and the jackdaws finalised their noisy plans overhead, both had reached for Brianna absentmindedly and found themselves hand in hand. So perfectly apt and so utterly natural was the instant that neither moved, each staring at the other in a state of true complicity. Mrs Root, glancing up from the range as she stirred the consommé, nodded contentedly to herself. "Thank the Lord for Miss Elinor," murmured the worthy woman, turning away tactfully as her ample cheeks flushed with recollections of her wayward teenaged years.

From "The Book of the City of Ladies"
by Christine de Pizan

"There is another greater and even more special reason for our coming which you will learn from our speeches: in fact we have come to vanquish from the world the same error into which you had fallen, so that from now on, ladies and all valiant women may have a refuge and defence against the various assailants, those ladies who have been abandoned for so long, exposed like a field without a surrounding hedge, without finding a champion to afford them an adequate defence, notwithstanding those noble men who are required by order of law to protect them, who by negligence and apathy have allowed them to be mistreated."

Chapter 6
Winter 1885, Kirtham:
A Happy Ending Planned

"I tell you I think it's fire. Air and light are required for its very survival. Maybe that's why so many wives are destined to live their lives in the cold."

"I see your point, really I do, but listen to me for just a minute. Why can't it be water? Life-giving, nourishing, cleansing and then, I admit, occasionally lethal in terms of drowning and flood damage."

"I shall not see this altercation as evidence of our non-compatibility. We're disputing at totally opposite ends of the spectrum, but may we find some common ground in that we both agree that it's natural, pray?"

"Absolutely. Why not? But wait a minute! I know, I have it! Why didn't I think of it before? It's nature plus time. We can compromise. It's stone!"

"…Unbreakable."

"I beg your pardon?"

"Never mind, go on, I like that, tell me why…"

Lively discussions surrounding the nature of love stretched long into the dreary winter days, taking the place of forestalled or abandoned exercise. While a stubborn sun settled low in the perpetually hoary sky, the lawns hardened into bleak little tundras, no man's lands crackling with hostility. In the garden, the trees stripped themselves painfully bare and let a sad silence rinse through their untenanted branches. Pauline was forced to fetch her easel upstairs, whereupon she and Nor as far as they were able immured themselves in the nursery by day, impregnable in their tiny sanctuary as they nurtured what must surely be fantastic plans for imminent flight beyond mere imagination. Robbed of the consolations of nature and inspired by Nor's evocative memories of home, paper seascapes fluttered from every inch of wall space, scenes of wild disparity from malevolent blue-black whirlpools spitting choppy surf to flat honey-coloured sands creamy with ruffled foam. As the topography of their surroundings altered, so did their attachment. Only there could dialogue season into discourse and discourse into the fervent mutual articulation of the unutterable.

One afternoon at the beginning of December Nor, wrapped in a woollen blanket and clearly out of sorts, leant at the narrow window, gazing apprehensively at an overcast sky marbling with heavy rain-bearing clouds in front of her eyes. She tip-toed over the crib to gaze at the sleeping child and tucked the blanket tighter around her twitching form. Then, selecting a piece of charcoal from the jar above the fireplace, she wrapped it tightly in Pauline's fingers, closing her own around her hand as together they traced a curling shape onto the parchment, circling whorls receding into a vanishing centre. Her voice, low and tender, told of fossils, relics hundreds of millions of years old and often shaped precisely like hairpins, if you please. Ammonites. They swirled the pencil faster around and around. Facing an inhospitable future, the resilient creatures had adapted and developed hard outer shells to protect themselves from predators. Impenetrable armour of their own making, second skins against calamity. And here was the astonishing part, once they had learned to defend themselves, the females evolved up to four times bigger than the males, she had seen them herself on Lyme Beach, majestic, coiled, forever fearless.

If Pauline's father had whiled away more than half of a highly contented century in his consideration of the happy ending, a new urgency pricked Nor and his daughter to dare if they could manufacture one for themselves and the little girl in their care. They agreed that Brianna's spell was already broken, her life foretold, there would be no pumpkin, no prince and no fairy godmother, if not for their intervention. Nor had snorted at the analogy. As far as she was concerned Cinderella was only ever confronted with two options and she was destined to be hobbled by both of them, dancing shoes or drudgery. Whatever they could contrive, they must do it within the scant remaining weeks of the nurse's sojourn, or the chance might never again present itself. Tonight, Kite would dine at the dairy with the Bits, a wedding had at last been negotiated and both families were keen to expedite proceedings before the prospective groom succumbed to his next malady. After a quiet supper in the kitchen, during which Mrs Root, solicitous but perceptive enough not to disturb the subdued atmosphere, dispensed lamb cutlets and soda bread with just the faintest of tuttings, they returned upstairs where their resolution wavered, the late hour shrouding the potential risks which, once conjured, assumed terrifying shapes, swarming out of the shadows into the stuttering light of a single candle flame as their conference grew fretful and uneasy.

They enjoyed one early advantage. Nor had requested an official interview with Kite to introduce the notion of Brianna attending the school in Lyme. She had secured the enthusiastic services of a renowned paediatric surgeon at The Infirmary, who promised to provide a robust endorsement of Nurse Budden's proposal which would serve as a reference. Being a clergyman, she went on to assure him, he would incur no fees and the establishment enjoyed a reputation for discretion, restoration and rehabilitation that was second to none. Kite had remained aloof and impassive throughout the interview, only allowing himself to chuckle as the nurse closed the door behind her. Better and better, he mused. Ambitious plans for the Rectory were at a crucial stage and he had been advised that the architectural and excavation work must start as soon as possible in early spring. Wisteria was to be ripped from the front of the house to make way for new Italianate stucco. Both the shabby apple trees and the wildflower meadow were scheduled for demolition ahead of the installation of an elegant water feature and parallel gravelled walks. With the changeling off the premises, and that interfering mountebank along with her, his wife could damned well do her duty and produce an heir worthy of his father's ambition. He was running out of patience with mistakenly locked doors, heavy colds that struck out of nowhere and 'Women's problems'. Let her limp back upstairs to her lunacy once she had answered to his needs and not before.

"What can I conceivably do? It's his right…"

"Wrong, it's his nature and what about your rights?"

"Nor, I am a wife!"

"You are a woman first! Can't you see? Men don't have to fight for independence or for freedom, so sometimes they just fight... You know what will become of you here, we both know it."

"He'll never let me go, never."

"We have to try. We can't not try."

Pauline had played so much fairer, as if that mattered now. She would permit minimal subterfuge, and on this they were had agreed. As above board as could be practically managed but surely her husband was not prepared to grant her extended leave to take their daughter south herself? The school would be obliged to assess Brianna's needs but Nor's sisters had already guaranteed that very few questions would be asked, and space could be made immediately to accommodate the girl. After that, let the rector try to take her back, even if he were to desire such a thing. The Buddens at Silver Street would become her family while they worked out what to do and the sea and sky would do the rest. The child was chaff in the wind to Kite, everyone knew it but his mulish grasp on his wife was if anything tighter than ever. In the end, miserable and exhausted, they could engineer no credible strategy that would enable them to leave Stonehaven together. Nor would journey with Brianna to Lyme after Christmas in her professional role as chaperone and then return immediately for Pauline. She would bring with her perhaps some semi-plausible excuse about the mother's on-site ratification of the child's treatment now being due and when they were both safely away, Kite would be forced to acknowledge the permanence of their absence. After that, their final destination remained uncertain, so long as it was far away from Kirtham.

Nor knew Pauline would never countenance it but the last resort must be blackmail; please God it wouldn't come to that but she had itemised a strictly scientific record of her patient's injuries since her arrival in the summer and she was hopeful that her medical testimony would carry some weight.

Just a few paltry weeks. What to do? How to prepare? It was unnervingly easy to obtain Kite's authorisation for a trip to Bicester, a reconnoitre of the train station and thorough examination of the seasonal timetable were sensible if the proposal was to execute itself efficiently. There were tickets to be booked and reservations to be made. He was almost fulsome in his acquiescence. Much easier to travel from there than to battle the crowds at Oxford but maybe they should journey to both and ask the advice of the station staff bearing in mind the holiday traffic they would be battling. The bracing air would do them all good and anyway Kite had important guests to entertain; the Baronet Dashwood was accompanying his very own garden designers to the Rectory to ascertain what could be done to make the environs halfway decent, shocking how the last incumbent had neglected the place. Ensure the fares were cheap, mind, no point squandering money on transport for staff.

The two women bundled Brianna up in knitted hat, scarf and mittens and trotted shivering into town next to Gideon East in the hard winter light, rattling along Oxford High to be deposited at the head of the alleyway that was Blue Boar Street. Since eight o'clock that morning Clara Pebble had pressed her angular face to the steaming window of the teashop in paroxysms of tingling anticipation. When guests arrived, despite a show of pink-tinged nonchalance, they were shown treatment worthy of royalty, nothing but the very best Chinese porcelain and fat slabs of brandy-soaked Christmas cake, the proportions of which drew puzzled and envious glances from the other customers. The eponymous proprietress was a fearsome woman of Amazonian proportions who sported a lopsided tartan turban and an expression of barely concealed rapaciousness. Parked permanently behind the till and given to quoting Millicent Garrett Fawcett at the big tippers as it rang piercingly out, she took a shine to Brianna and by association Nor and Pauline, filling their teapot free for the second time and assuring them abstrusely that courage spoke to courage alright sisters, but that Clara had best get her scrawny wee backside behind the counter, for sure the Battenbergs wouldn't slice themselves! Indeed, the morning had been spent so very enjoyably that a rare optimism warmed them all the journey home, despite the onslaught of a thin, greasy rain.

The next morning, they enjoyed a brisk excursion to Bicester, which proved the more expedient of starting points due not only to its proximity but also to its strategic position ensuring a seat on the train ahead of the throngs at Oxford. Trundling back along the lanes towards Kirtham, the dutiful East was compelled to exercise caution; a treacherous sprinkling of frost was even now dusting the verges, and the first signs of snow mobilised in the blade-sharp breeze. In the back of the gig, a sympathetic Nor was listening to tales of Mr Barnaby and Dr Belshire, how they had sustained Pauline through unbearable bereavement, how they had been expunged forcibly from her life and how she felt like an important part of herself was always missing, like a single glove on a park bench. Yesterday's memories of Oxford had brought them back to her in all their splendid sincerity and her mood was downcast once more as they crunched up the driveway. Alerting Mrs Root to their return, Nor admitted that she had twice spied Dr Belshire's distinguished silver head among a sea of expectant and respectful student faces during his Infirmary visits. She still intended to speak to him as soon as the opportunity presented itself and agreed he managed to project at all times an aura both approachable and illustrious.

Inside, the temperature plummeted lower still as Kite uncoiled from his study like a cobra seething with unmitigated fury. Corporal Osian Jones, he hissed in a deadly whisper, had departed the premises, marching away for good, direction Canterbury on a mission all his own. His parting words were all in praise of Nurse Budden, a "living visionary" so he said, credited with having inspired his campaign to the holy places of Britain. His was a heavily edited version of the fusilier's unflattering valediction. Before he left, Jones had made so bold as to share with the churchman a short homily on pride and a confession that he, like Jones, might after all have misjudged the gentler sex. His parting shot had been to proclaim in his velvet rasp that all is vanity as he swaggered around the bend, raising his cap in a final jaunty salute, 'Onward Christian Soldiers' lingering in the freezing air like an imprecation. Kite ordered the mute removed upstairs immediately. Meanwhile, with his wife in attendance, he subjected Nor to a searingly reproachful tirade, ending in dismissal effective immediately, or at least first thing tomorrow morning, weather notwithstanding; be sure she would take the child with her, the very least she could do before resuming her place at The Infirmary, provided they required her services after the coruscating complaint he intended to make to her superiors. He sincerely hoped this would be their last conversation. Mrs Kite would now accompany him without delay, and he presumed he had made abundantly clear that he considered the matter closed. Nearly choking with rage as he spat out the final syllables, he dabbed at his upper lip with a square of carnelian silk and, clenching his fist, jerked his arm abruptly outwards in an irrefutable invitation to Pauline who was pulled upstairs without having uttered a single word.

It was only towards six that morning that she and Nor could spend a snatched moment together. Horrified, both had been stunned by the actuality of premature estrangement. In the porch, Kite snarled orders at Gideon East who was still yawning and pulling on his jacket over what looked like a thread bare nightshirt, while upstairs the nurse knelt in front of Pauline, sitting bolt upright by the cooling grate, her red-gold head low in her hands and her beautiful mouth twisted with grief. She roused herself as she felt her slim shoulders enveloped in the soft blue nursing cape, Nor's trembling finger tracing the faint pulse at the base of her throat as lightly as the clasp was fixed firmly under her chin that Pauline thought she might have imagined it through sheer force of her shattered will.

"There's nothing else I can leave with you to make you believe me. Take it. This is me – it's who I am. Keep it with you, hold it close to you, feel me with you. They won't part us. I will look after her and I will come back for you, I promise." As she passed over her daughter and with her all the hope and hunger she had so long suppressed, Pauline's eyes shone black against the dying embers. Outside, a darkly pensive East was stowing Nor's trunk in the gig for the return to Bicester Station, he considered it inhuman to take to the roads in these bitter conditions. There was kind old Mrs Root, indignant in pinny and cap, steaming out of the pantry door, disapproval hardened in her eye, Brianna limp in her voluminous embrace. The bairn was barely recognisable, bent almost double over a small horse of walnut wood that East had whittled himself; perhaps she was singing softly to herself but then again, she could be keening. The howling winds whipped words away and ice-melt soaked their clothes. Before they were swept up in the whirling snow, Nor battled vainly with herself convinced, as she was sure Eurydice had been before her, that looking back was the worst thing she could do even as she craned her neck for a final glimpse before the house was walled up in white. Kite's erect figure was framed in the front door in the act of slamming it shut, a sneer upon his handsome features as he waggled his fingers theatrically at the departing vehicle. Pauline she could not discern, but high at the top of the house what looked like a perfect square of artic blue at the window seemed to signal the way to freedom, like a patch of bright sky after a storm or a hole blown in the wall of a fortress.

From "Dover Beach"
by Matthew Arnold

Ah, love, let us be true
to one another! For the world, which seems
to lie before us like a land of dreams,
So various, so beautiful, so new,
Hath really neither joy, nor love, nor light,
Nor certitude, nor peace, nor help for pain…

Chapter 7
Winter 1885
Kirtham and Lyme Regis:
Success and Catastrophe

Thoroughly dazed and heartsore, Nor nonetheless endured the interminable journey stoically, watching the landscape beyond the breath-fogged windows transition from dark, silt-slagged warehouses to the frost-tipped chocolate browns of the rural ploughlands through a mist of indistinct pain, shaken from her melancholy from time to time by a highly animated Brianna who showed no signs of fatigue although night had not long ended. At Bicester station, numb with shock and more than a little daunted, she had nevertheless baulked at third class, horrified by the exposed wooden cattle-truck which passed as accommodation for the poorer passengers, settling instead for second-class tickets which had cost her a month's wages. They were sorely unprepared for the change at Reading but settled in by Basingstoke after some confusion at as to the appropriate line to Yeovil. Nor was so thoroughly exhausted simply ensuring the safety of her small charge and keeping the measly luggage together that she snapped automatically into the efficient functionality of Nurse

Budden; she would allow herself no access to emotions lest she find herself incapable of the simplest of actions. Brianna must be her priority now, until her security was assured, she would not acknowledge her own wretchedness. All that raw winter's day they travelled, huddled together on benches in shabbily upholstered booths through the penumbral lunchtime gloom and much later, on the tiny local locomotive to the small market town of Bridport, coughing and hawking through streaming eyes as the viscous fumes of an oil lamp dangling precariously from the ceiling spiralled through their all but empty carriage.

The dregs of Nor's snatched savings afforded the man hour in a hired pony and trap, in which they rattled the last six miles to Lyme through the early twilight. Breasting the hill at Uplyme, a faint fluttering ribbon in the sky darkened into a line of Canada geese rippling energetically towards the coast. At her first glance of the sombre sea, foxed like a mirror and the same silver-grey, Brianna's green eyes sparkled. She scrambled up to get a closer look, leaning perilously close to the edge of the crude vehicle, feet scrabbling for purchase in the frigid air. All day long she had stubbornly refused to relinquish either Nor's hand or the little wooden horse and now the skittish driver, a sad-faced, downy-lipped boy given to vigorous rubbing at the rash of purple pustules bristling on his neck had been forced to stop at the side of the road and tie her onto the seat with a length of dirty bailer twine.

He left them at the bottom of Silver Street as darkness fell, clip-clopping off towards the Ship Inn and the dilemma of beer or a bed for the night. It was with some consternation that Nor pulled along her now weary little charge before halting outside the wonky paint-flaked windows halfway up the slope. Inside, she could just make out Mam, frizzy grey hair awry, grinning mid-laugh, up to her elbows in suet and there was Pa, whiter about the beard for sure, and surely a little stouter, tinkering with an ancient lobster net before a cheerful fire. Tapping on the pane, she eased open the door and the two of them fairly tumbled in, her parents already smiling and raising their arms in an invitation to embrace ahead of a homecoming she knew would be joyous however unprepared for. As expected, Pa Budden was ecstatic to see his first-born child and swept her into brawny arms, tousling her hair just as he would a son's and chuckling as she inhaled the fishy, briny scent of him like she was practising how to breathe. Mam was already fussing around the child, who was quaking with cold and muttering, letting her lick the spoon before cooing and ahhing at her curly head – "Just like October beeches, right, Pa?" Even as she reached for the pan to warm some milk with just a touch of vanilla sugar and a sprinkle of allspice. The toddler was causing a right bustle and flap, to the point of being awarded one of Mam's coveted bottled peaches, a ceremony Nor remembered only witnessing twice before and which involved Pa balancing a thick dictionary on top of a stool to reach the dust-covered jar atop the bookcase. Soon enough, Brianna had nodded off, lodged in a truckle bed squeezed tight under the stairs, still clutching her wooden toy and whickering happily as Blighter, the Buddens' Jack Russell, carried out his designated duty as official bed warmer.

Moments later, Nor's two pretty sisters bustled in with the first feathery flakes of snow sliding off their tip-tilted noses, shedding colourful ribbons and wielding quantities of brown paper. They squealed in unison when they caught sight of her collapsed on the settle. A surprise half-day holiday had prompted a quick foray to the general store just as it was closing. The two were returning from their labours at the school. An unprecedented decision had been reached that very day to close the establishment simply for Christmas Day itself, so great was the demand for their practical philanthropy. They admired little Brianna in her cot, put their arms around their sister and commented not at all upon her pale complexion and her red, swollen eyes. Neither did they share with her the news that Mam was just recovered from a bout of shingles, nor that Pa's sciatica was flaring worse than ever. Naturally, the family had been informed by Nor herself about her facial injuries although they had never seen them for themselves. One fine, dark line like a wayward hair stuck to her right cheek was all that remained of the seamstress' farewell and to the Buddens it would always wear the seal and stamp of a war-wound honourably suffered. Harriet and Flora, twins in every sense of the word, simply confirmed for each other and stored away against a discussion at a later date the fact that their sibling was just as forthright as she had always been albeit tonight somewhat solemn and uncharacteristically hushed. No mention was made of either her unscheduled appearance or the lack of signature blue cape which they had never known their sister to be without; long familiarity and some inexplicable chemical coordination between the two suggested that an answer would not be forthcoming.

Eventually, and with palpable reluctance, Mam and Pa traipsed drowsily off to bed as a raucous wind arose out in the bay bringing with it flurries of grittier snow, battering the house and shaking the casements. Plans were made between the girls for an introduction to the principal of the charitable

99

school on the morrow, the mention of whom resulted in a modest blush creeping up Flora's throat and much mirth between the other sisters. It had all been arranged, Brianna would be seated next to Jonah Bye, the chandler's boy. He was the brightest and friendliest of them all, his was the straightest back in the county, never mind that his wasted legs had been in callipers from the age of two. He would look after her. They had that very morning finished her pinafore, embroidered with a bumbler chasing round a buttercup above a sunshine-yellow 'B'. Did she know that Pa had spent the last fortnight fashioning a pair of soft canvas boots for her which were lined with rabbit fur? The rest of the evening was spent in nostalgic childhood recollections of Christmases gone by until Nor could keep awake no longer and crept up to her old bedroom on the rickety third floor only to toss and turn in painful contemplation of how the happiest of homecomings rendered so hard the journey she had still to make. The temptation to stay was almost overwhelming but her heart was already elsewhere and when her mother had discreetly suggested that a problem shared, love... all she could answer was "Not this time, Mam".

The next day, the whole family made the expedition through the watery sunshine to the local school, distributing a mountain of hot biscuits among the infants and taking tea with the very agreeable Parson Joseph Gennifer, a nice-looking, rather ordinary man who had rendered himself exceptional through humility and benevolence, but who found himself sadly unequal to concealing his blatant admiration for Flora. His integrity and his natural talents in instruction, most notably religious and historical, were secondary in Nor's view to his growing reputation as a chronicler of Dorset's flora and fauna, along with detailed and quite astonishingly adept sketches which Pauline herself would be hard put to better. Brianna seemed to have her mother in mind too, scratching out a very credible robin in colourful chalk on the playground pavement along with two other little girls. Gennifer declared himself charmed and more than ready to accommodate the child from tomorrow; Miss Flora herself would take charge of the programme and he would be very surprised if she hadn't got the mite quoting Dryden by Easter, compassionate pedagogy being her very special gift. Even Mam had squirmed. After lunch, Nor secreted herself in her room to compose the message, worded precisely as they had agreed, that communicated not only Brianna's safe, permanent and happy assimilation but her own renewed vow to fetch Pauline before Christmas. Harriet, suspecting nothing, had been only too happy to take dictation to address the already sealed envelope and the letter to a Mrs Root at Kirtham Rectory was dispatched without delay, the first part of its journey expedited on a steam cart loaded with Blue Lias bound for Dorchester.

Was hubristic confidence that there remained sufficient time for a reunion to blame for what happened next? Not even Nurse Budden could have foreseen the cruel and untimely fever that would take possession of her during her second night in Lyme. She was in and out of consciousness as midnight came and went, acknowledging only her father's solicitous expression and a warm, scented cloth draped around her forehead before the dark took over again. Tireless and dedicated, Harriet and Flora nursed her through that night and the next and the next, the days taking them away to their educational duties while Mam and Pa looked on and ministered to her as they might a new-born. After nearly a week, the sisters assured them that Nor's temperature was near enough to normal and that she had managed a mouthful of bone broth in the small hours. Puzzling to all of them thought was that Nor, as if in defiance of regaining her damaged health day by day, seemed if anything more distressed now than during her mercifully brief illness. Still, she kept her own counsel and secretly longed to be gone. Almost a week lost! And yet she knew she was too weak to undertake the long trip back to Kirtham in the near future. The torpor of forced recuperation continued to sap her spirits while time seemed to sprint by, its blinding white days and disorienting black nights conspiring against her.

The child, meanwhile, had assumed her position both in the Budden household and at the school with infectious delectation. She and Jonah were soon like brother and sister, each displaying a candid consideration for the other while innocent flirtation and friendly competition informed many of their interactions. Brianna proved instinctively kind, sharing lunches with the poor boy which would form almost mythologised memories in the future; bread and dripping, sausage scraps and golden onions, leftover wedges of fragrant game pie. The sounds which emanated from her smiling mouth were as yet unintelligible but she was a rare conversationalist, and if confidence alone were an indicator, she might soon be in position to pronounce her favourite monosyllable, 'Sea'. If the elements permitted it, the high point of her days after instruction and play was a trip with her 'Aunts' to the beach, on which Brianna would execute for them all the same unselfconscious solemn jig, holding aloft her two small hands towards the water like she was administering a blessing and wriggling her whole body to unheard music. The Budden sisters were encouraged by her progress and in awe of what they considered an artist's interpretive spirit. "You're quite right, Brianna." Harriet nodded, her blue eyes kindly. "The sea is shaking; it's exactly like a dance; sometimes a gentle pas de deux when it's feeling sleepy…"

"And sometimes a fierce fandango when it's angry!" finished Flora, hoisting Brianna onto her hip and spinning her around. Amid much laughter, they hurried back to Silver Street to start the ceremony of tree decoration and mistletoe garlanding, for tomorrow was Christmas Eve.

So, when the family woke to Nor's cold bed and unaccountable absence spirits were crushed to say the least. Amid wild suppositions and unwarranted recriminations, her sisters discovered a note under her pillow merely clarifying that one imperative duty remained to her and that she trusted they would understand and explain to their dear parents that she would see them all again very soon. And please to promise Mam that the hole in the housekeeping money would be patched within the week. She had slipped out at first light with just a handheld satchel she had stowed unseen the previous evening behind Brianna's bed. Unbeknownst to her, amongst her hurriedly packed clothes and other rudimentaries there nestled the wooden horse, wedged amongst her belongings by a small nocturnal hand so that the toy might at least try to provide her with some cheerful company wherever she might be headed.

Nor had strategically departed the house in time to beg a ride with the caravan of drays en route to Yeovil market, an experience she knew she would never forget; the close-knit fraternity of local farmers and fishermen was kindness itself to Budden's oldest girl, sharing their breakfast of crisp hot baked potatoes, which they showed her how to arrange in her pockets to best keep herself warm for the three quarters of the way, at which point pats of fresh gold butter appeared wrapped in coarse linen and frothy beer was dispensed from thick, cool earthenware jars. She relished their cheerful company and was genuinely sorry when, in perfect union, they yodelled a tuneful farewell and swung the wagons smartly around the corner of the train station like a flock summoned by the shepherd's dog.

By the time she had regained Oxford, she felt less dizzy and more determined, in spite of her aching back and drumming temples. However, it soon became apparent that the train would not be advancing to Bicester as scheduled and indeed the passengers were summarily ordered to quit the vehicle while an extra coach was fastened, to make room for the Christmas crowds. Out on the chilly concourse she realised just how teeming the place was and for a second, wavered in her decision to keep going. Bodies pressed in on all sides, brightly wrapped gifts stabbing her in the stomach and scattered children treading on her toes in a good-natured frenzy. Ready to surrender and shoulder her way out to seek alternative transport, she rooted in her satchel for her ticket, finding instead Brianna's toy and clutching it tightly to her, suddenly misty-eyed. Just then Nor caught sight of a familiar face at the far end of the platform and raised the little horse reflexively in greeting before dipping down again to rescue her bag, even now knocking its way through the surging droves almost onto the tracks. Mr Choudhry had spotted her at almost the same time and smiled warmly in mutual recognition, although his first feeling registered as one of perturbation. The delightful Nurse Budden and her little ward, for surely she was bending to retrieve the child from the bustling scrum, must have been turned away from the school and be on their way back to Kirtham in defeat. How tiresome but maybe they were precipitous in their plan for enrolment, the recommendation could not have arrived yet from The Infirmary. Barred from approaching any closer by the sheer seething mass of humanity, they lost sight of each other and separately joined the casual observers as the surplus compartment, screeching like a soul in purgatory, was hitched to the still-snorting locomotive. Thereafter, the apothecary was borne by the assembly into this same accommodation at the rear while Nor was swept up the platform to a forward car behind the engine. Once it had pulled out of the station, the congested vehicle's exertions persisted both deafening and nauseating, the unholy screams of the whistle interspersed only by swarming effusions of soot and cinders which floated gaily back into the cars, blown through the gaps and cracks, settling in the passengers' eyes, noses and hair irrespective of class.

Soon they were making their way through rural pastures approaching Kidlington. There was a different kind of snow here, Nor noticed idly, less luxurious, more brittle, essentially a scrape of bluish ice over the landscape as far as the eye could see, silver-tipped fields, freckled fences and pearly skies shimmering through the skeletal branches of long-established winter trees. Agitated and restive, she was relieved to yield up her precious seat to a harassed-looking young mother and her bawling son, a fractious boy who was immediately placated by the horse that Nor surrendered to him, gnawing at one of the stubby wooden legs, refusing thereafter to part with it.

Resigned, she shuffled further back down the train, crossing the connecting gangway between the carriages with care. There was no peace to be had anywhere, clattering windows and singing drafts, carousing passengers passing a bottle of sloe gin round as they mangled a carol or two. Glancing up, her attention was momentarily riveted by a man all in black waving his hat out of the rearmost hatch before a sharp-angled turn prevented her from studying him further. It couldn't be Choudhry, could it? She attempted to pull down the window cord, but frost had stuck it fast. All at once, a tremendous lurch nearly tipped her onto the floor. Grabbing the door handle to right herself, she emitted an involuntary yelp as the glacial steel all but removed the skin from her fingers.

At the back of the train, Choudhry had been ruminating reciprocally on Nurse Budden and considering how best to approach the tricky rector to suggest a second attempt be made to settle the child at a good educational facility. His thoughts wandered; he considered it only fitting, given the disheartening news about his wife's visa detention in Paris and his wasted journey to London, that he had fetched up in this, a barely disguised third-class boneshaker put on for holidaymakers. In fact, he appreciated the irony that nothing seemed to be going his way recently. And that's where his reflections ceased, abruptly and without warning. A deafening, high-pitched metallic shriek, followed by an agonising series of sharp jolts and a sickening lunge were all he could recollect as the entire rear compartment, creakily venerable and hastily coupled by overtired staff, detached itself, slowing ponderously for a few seconds before leaving the rails altogether and dropping onto its side, picking up speed as it slid down a shallow bank and skated along the icy turf. Eventually, after what seemed like hours, it dragged to a protracted stop like a wounded beast trailing dirty great smears in the snow.

The passengers up front were none the wiser as the locomotive swung nonchalantly around a bend and chugged along the top of an embankment adjacent to the Cherwell River. From her tactical vantage point in front of the window, Nor suddenly found herself perfectly positioned to glimpse simultaneously the church of St Giles in the hamlet of Hampton Gay and that of The Holy Cross in the village of Shipton if she turned her head sharply enough. Her heart lightened as the two stately towers came into view, sharply delineated against the crisp winter sky but in that instant the labouring train appeared to change its mind about its direction of travel as it topped the bridge; it braked wildly, shuddering, seemed to shake itself down like a shivering dog for two or three tantalising seconds then swung decisively off the tracks and plunged down the steep escarpment, sending spinning all three remaining carriages over and over as they collided in turn with the buckled iron railings and pitched head long into the freezing slush. Her last memories were of muddled senses melding, all indicating danger and all too late. As a grinding banshee scream of tearing steel rent the winter air, she stared aghast while a pristine swan, startled mid-landing, slammed ricocheting into the glass, scattered scarlet Rowan berries from the hedgerows stuttering across the water like bullets; she only had time to wonder what shade of red Pauline would call them before everything went dark.

Later, the newspapers would lead for weeks with headlines about 'carriages smashed to atoms' and partial bodies unidentifiable in the brackish melt water. An Oxford professor had contributed to an article calculating the odds of survival when soft tissue came into contact with undiscriminating arbitrary shards of metal, concluding that, given the addition of deep water and fuel-based fire, the result was an infinitely doomed algorithm. While the emergency services were quickly mobilised and generous aid immediately proffered from such elevated quarters as nearby Blenheim Palace and the Manor House at Hampton, it emerged that Choudhry and most of his fellow passengers had escaped miraculously intact, if bloodied and bruised, some succumbing in immobile shock to mild hypothermia and others galvanised into action alongside the rescue teams, if only in search of distraction from the emerging horror. Heavily bandaged, his head sporting a shallow contusion and his left arm in a sling, the apothecary aligned himself with the latter cohort, wandering dazed and tearful among the apocalyptic scenes in a hopeless search for Nurse Budden and little Brianna. Hieronymus Bosch could not have done justice to the scenes of nightmarish distortions that the accident had spawned. Ducks paddled insouciantly in and out of the engine's ruined carcass while one of the deformed carriages reared bolt upright as if hurled out of a toy box in a tantrum. On impact, the flames had set to work, licking through the exposed timbers, igniting leaking diesel fumes and spraying lethal sparks more than fifty yards in every direction but now an eerie silence prevailed, aside from a sinister, percussive drip and hiss. Behind hastily erected barriers he saw fire crews and medics scurrying casualties out of the charred wreckage, checking wearily for signs of life. The nearby paper mill at Hampton was turned into a temporary mortuary to house the burgeoning pile of corpses which flattened the reeds along the riverbank, stretchers bearing away the injured to The Infirmary in Oxford. Choudhry, in ever-deepening despair, came eventually to rest supporting a fire fighter whose awful pallor rendered him twice ghostly in the snow, his good arm stretched around the youth's muscled shoulders as the lad sobbed uncontrollably, cradling in his blackened hand the sooty, charred remains of what he called "some poor moppet's little wooden donkey" before he fainted clean away.

The choppy breeze subsided to leave a turbid miasma of smoke and fumes. When the Reverend Aubrey Kite materialised out of the fog, Choudhry seriously assumed he was hallucinating and wondered if he had sustained more than just a superficial head injury. The cleric had been swiftly summoned to administer to the dead and dying in his role as vicar in charge of Akeman Benefice of which the tiny St Giles was a member. Picking his way through the reeking carnage with a black kerchief held delicately to his nose, Kite recognised the apothecary at once and automatically offered his condolences while Choudhry delivered with mournful conviction the news of the demise of the inestimable Nurse Budden, presumably on her way back from Lyme in one of the condemned carriages from which no survivors had emerged. Assuming an expression of suitable gravity, Kite indicated the sign of the cross and made to move on, but clearly the man hadn't finished yet. What he heard next put to the test every vestige of Kite's long-mastered artfulness, and by the time he had finished heeding the dreadful tidings of the death of his only child a makeshift seat had swiftly been constructed and a tincture of rum produced for the bereaved clergyman.

Afternoon stiffened into evening and then froze solid into a searingly cold night before Kite could decently attempt a return to Kirtham. He had been much admired, his benedictions and consolations warmly received, and his reputation bolstered by his seemingly spontaneous poetic solemnities. On reaching the Rectory some time just before midnight, he bounded straight up the stairs and into Pauline's chamber, wresting her roughly from her bed and lighting the candle as he peeled off his gloves and shook out his sodden cloak. This was a happy ending of which her old father would be proud, he crowed, squatting on the edge of her bed and wrapping his arm firmly round her waist as he dispensed with formalities, baldly stating that despite a tedious and decidedly uncomfortable evening, two deaths in this tragedy were decidedly of some personal interest. Pauline's gaze flickered in the half-light as he breezed on, tightening his grip as he related the details of the night's experience. Would she credit it but that incompetent nurse had managed not only to have their offspring refused entry to the school, but she had also worked her magic in ensuring that while scuttling shamefully home again the two of them suffered the most horrible deaths in a train wreck in the middle of nowhere. There came no reaction. He raised his eyebrows, demanding a response. His wife had always had the capacity to unnerve him but now she floored him completely and for the first time he felt a little fearful. He had just informed her that her darling daughter was no more and yet her face remained completely expressionless, betraying if anything a trace of triumph in the uplift of her chin as her fathomless eyes finally met his. He dropped his arm as if scalded and gaped at her in disbelief while she unhurriedly removed her nightcap, shook out her glowing

110

titian hair and plaited it carefully into its simple braid, at length succumbing to tears and turning away from him.

A mere four miles away, Nor Budden lay unconscious on a hard wooden cot in The Boat Inn at Thrupp, a tiny village just across the fields from the site of the accident. The canal-side dwellers had thrown opened their doors to harbour the injured as best they could until hospital accommodation could be located for those lucky enough to have escaped with their lives. She was talked of as a rare miracle; such a strong young woman, she must have been close to a splintered door or broken window to be flung free of the wreck, a serendipitous blessing indeed. Make no mistake, her injuries were grievous: initial assessments included severe concussion, two broken ankles, and a shattered collarbone. Unnamed and unrecognised, no identification had been discovered on her broken body; no-one was contacted, and nobody informed of her whereabouts. As another black dawn broke over the site of the worst rail disaster in living memory, a solitary swan circled endlessly around and around the stack of crumpled debris in a demented loop, as if searching for something not quite irretrievably lost.

From "Power in Silence"
by Michael Field

Though I sing high, and chaunt above her,
Praising my girl,
It were not right
To reckon her the poorer lover;
She does not love me less
For her royal, jewelled speechlessness,
She is the sapphire, she the light,
The music in the pearl.

Chapter 8
Fragments of Pauline Kite's
Chiaroscuro Diaries

24 February 1884–Dark

What might constitute my fate were he to stumble upon these intermittent writings I dare not consider and yet these three years past, I must confess to a kind of perverse stimulation wrought by the dread of their discovery. By this, I know that I am still alive. How I muster the wherewithal – I cannot call it courage, audacity perhaps? – to execute them, I cannot say but I should surrender entirely to inertia without the distraction that they afford and after all, fear and I are no strangers. Since my marriage, I have suffered a systematic slicing away of all that is good in my life. I employ the combination of adjective and verb advisedly; my husband is never niggardly in the regular distribution of his barbarity all, apparently, for our mutual experiential benefit. And yet, while I abhor his weakness and shudder at his touch, I cannot bring myself to despise him utterly, for I consider him the unhappiest human being I have ever encountered. His wretchedness consumes him, avarice and its crooked double, disappointment, riding on each shoulder like wolfish little devils. A profane composite of the cabal at the Villa Diodati, Father would no doubt label him. Agreed, he possesses Lord Byron's insatiable allure and Mary Shelley's words '*I had cast off all feeling, subdued all anguish, to riot in the excess of my despair. Evil thenceforth became my good*' could have been written or him. What is it that would bring him satisfaction? Status, money, women, wine? I cannot accurately venture. In his more philosophical moments, my husband professes that I am his blessed consolation; it is simple physics, he advises me, the more pain I bear, the sweeter his relief and the more brio he is thence at liberty to sprinkle on his days. He explains all this like an eager young schoolmaster, so dreadfully handsome, bright eyes ablaze in inverse proportion to the ugliness of his nefarious passions. If I knew no better, I should suspect that Laudanum plays a part in maintaining the sharp edge of his yet famished proclivities. So, dear Father, I would interpret him more accurately as Polidori's Ruthven, but rather than sucking my blood, he thrives on making an exhaustive study of it. Thus, he grows stronger and I weaker in a pernicious mockery of marital symbiosis.

When we removed to Kirtham from my beloved Oxford, I allowed myself some faint hope of reprieve. How naïve that seems now. While he continues to bask in his newfound distinction and the elevated company that his cronies at the park provide, this grand house and its grounds grants him continued licence to all but sequester me from public view. As my parameters continue to shrink, I begrudge even Melmoth his ability to roam, for my bones are turning to dust but to whom can I appeal? The proliferating rumours both of my diminishing mental capacity and our daughter's unlucky disfigurement ensure that the villagers are reluctant to call; I hear the servants talk. Here in the wide-open country, I am less at liberty than ever and neither need my injuries conceal themselves under the gloves or skirts that town necessitates. Instead, my husband grows gleefully enterprising. So far, he spares the child but dear God, for how long? I will not taint her name by bringing it among these pages; I fear for her future but lack the means to do more than pray.

Today, pain has rendered itself part of my biology; I can no longer remember a time before its chronic and persistent accompaniment, mundane these days as air, inhaled even as isolation and loneliness corrupt it, mushrooming through my lungs like a contagion. It wastes me, whittles my confidence, re-fashions me as a withered shade, a spectre. I am all but mute these days. Aside from these sporadic diaries, drawing is my only means of expression but who will ever mark these images and translate them into meaning? Do they even signify? These are the scattered remnants of me, and I may never be made whole again. Yesterday, in high spirits, my husband bound a kerchief around my eyes to obscure vision and disorient before he spun me around three times and connected the heel of his hand with my left cheekbone. In the interests of anatomical and artistic enquiry, I am confined to the grounds for week; I must communicate with no-one and wear my veil until I am fit again. My contribution is to produce as lifelike a rendition as I am able after a period of three days so that he might evaluate his skill against mine in the spirit of friendly rivalry.

1 December 1884–Light

He is from home for today at least and perhaps tomorrow! I must dash my thoughts down now, before they dissolve, before quotidian cares intrude. I am more at ease today than I have been in many weeks. I awoke from a vivid dream of my brother and have held him close in my heart throughout the morning. He is so like our mother was, not just in his handsome physical resemblance but in his humour, his optimism and his ability genuinely to find gratification in the enthusiastic participation of daily life. He never fails to cheer me. In my present frame of mind, I relish more than ever conundrums and anomalies; I honestly consider his estrangement a prize, his banishment a triumph and his continued absence marks the very zenith of my accomplishments. He is alive, far from here and out of reach. God watch over him wherever he be; one day I know we shall be reunited.

While I am counting my meagre blessings, I see that I am not as unremittingly alone as I at first feared. I am reminded of the child Clara and how we practised a mutually sustaining empathy towards the end of our time in Oxford. I am sure I can discern the beginnings of such a liaison with Mrs R. What a genuinely adorable creature, so giving, warm and infinitely charitable; a true Christian woman! I cannot hold against her that she remains woefully ignorant of the nature and extent of her employer's depravities; she continues a discreet and sympathetic support to me and during his more frequent absences, our genuine regard and gentle affinity reminds me of old times at St John's. Today, she toiled to the top of the house to proclaim that she had concocted a batch of my favourite Brown Windsor; I, in return, lent her my copy of

Braddon's 'Serpent', knowing her love of sensation. She vouched to debate a full analytical comparison with her beloved Collins before the New Year but doubted he could be matched for sheer deliciousness! Tomorrow we shall walk out together to the kitchen garden to inspect the progress of Mr East's winter vegetables ahead of the Christmas preparations. Her devotion to the wellbeing of my child warms my heart and she, along with her loyal, grizzled retainer, provides me with much-needed cheer in these dark days. I shall chart my course to the kitchen at every opportunity, for there legitimate friendship lies.

The other event worthy of note was the impromptu appearance this afternoon of the amiable Mr Choudhry. He elucidated most convincingly his own theory regarding my persistent low spirits. To wit, the circumstances of my mother's grievous death have defiled my own experience of parenthood by association. He suggested that I attempt to exorcise my lassitude by applying myself to the development of my creative art, which he greatly admires and the education of my daughter, whom he declares shall be my salvation. Mrs R sat chaperone and when he learned by way of casual conversation of my husband's removal, he became at once positively loquacious on the subject of female health, reporting unequivocally but with customary tact the horrors he had witnessed during his training in an Indian sanatorium where melancholic mothers were treated with shocks, bloodletting, burning, Mercury and antimony when all that was needed, in his opinion, were the vitamins provided by our own sunlight, compassion and time to heal. I appreciate his chilling warning to me, although naturally I could not acknowledge it. Taking his leave, he proudly quoted John

Donne, exhorting me to "Breathe, shine and seek to mend" as he swept off the porch with a bow, brushing past the rustling holly which seemed to echo the same refrain.

Even on this intensely cold day, I can call to mind traces of what makes me glad: cut grass, liquorice, Cosi fan Tutti and the verse of Aphra Behn. This momentary respite revives my failing senses; tonight, I shall take to bed the woodpecker's scintillating peridot blaze and the rough silk of teasels on my fingers. Maybe there is meaning in the world. I remember the last time I beheld dear Dr Belshire that harsh winter some years ago, he recounted to me the astonishing tale of the young somnambulist Miss Dalrymple, whose deathly fall was broken at the last conceivable minute by the most banal of providences. Perhaps we should never surrender our faith in intervention, mortal or divine. Today, anything is possible and the freedoms of the heart and of the mind seem limitless. Today, I consider my husband wrong to dismiss me as infirm. The apothecary is right; I have endured the intimate and complex pangs of birth and know that I am strong.

28 March 1885 – Darker

Despite spring at long last beckoning beneath my window, my spirits falter in the glare of returning sunlight. I lack the mental sinew to regain the smallest scrap of my former hope and not even dear Mrs R can penetrate the depths of my despair. Resorting to self-seclusion, I am cocooned up here with my daughter day in and day out. Often, I sleep, most of the time I close my eyes and remember. The past is a safer place to be, the present petrifies me. The forces of my destiny are gathering and naturally I am impotent against them. I recognise all the terms: post-partum depression, hysteria, puerperal insanity, cerebral congestion. But I, a woman who is punished for each enunciated syllable with stringent exactitude, cannot remonstrate. Growing up, I used to value silence, considered it a rare virtue, but now it seems to masquerade as madness after all. How has no-one noticed the uncomplicated truth? I am not mad; I am simply in constant distress. I am not ill, ergo I require no diagnosis. There is very much a sequence of cause and effect to be ascertained if only someone would take the time to trace it. Kill the cause and the symptoms will die along with it. I suffer regular mental and physical torture, I am hideously lonely, intellectually and emotionally deprived all these things can be reversed. Instead, at twenty-four, I grow old.

The papers tell of the repulsive 'moral insanity' pertaining to unfaithful wives but my husband returns home trailing lavender and jasmine and proceeds to preach the homily without blinking. Toothless against legislation which favours men and belittles women, those same laws cause me to be ostracised, demonised and humiliated. Why? Because one similarly bright spring day a lifetime ago, I married a monster. It was all too easy and I, an educated and intelligent woman, appear to have signed my life away to an aficionado of cruelty like some poor, pathetic Mrs Quilp.

5 August 1885 – Lighter

Ma always held that time was relative, that our feeble human comprehension of it will always be absurdly reductive. It is summer, and so much has changed. This afternoon, N looked straight at me and saw, must have seen, an affirmation in my eyes which granted consent. Gently, she laid her cool hand on my forehead, and what happened next took me by surprise; a flicker of warmth, a sprite beneath the skin transformed what I mistook for sympathy and ignited a flame which licked along my spine and flourished in my cheeks. And I realised then that I look for her, around the house. I seek her everywhere, her shape, her sound, the long curve of her back and her strolling, loping stride. All the songs, all the poems, all the novels are true. I catch my breath, and I struggle to maintain my upright posture, my attitude which has become second nature to me here. I am aloof, I cultivate froideur. I counterfeit. Mrs R thinks I have the beginnings of a fever and I do; I do. Whatever I see, taste, feel and explore: I am thinking she would understand this better than me, I must remember to tell her about this and show her that and we can learn about them together. These thoughts cross my mind before I remember that there is no us, no imagined future. How could there ever be? There's a kind of obscenity in the everyday where in the truth has no place. Solitude no longer comforts me, I am simply adrift, a lonely place and so far from her. All I desire is to utter the words "I love you" and all I can do is swallow them down and unlearn them. Today, I ponder Othello's plaintive reasoning, "Though that her jesses were my dear heartstrings, I'd whistle her off and let her down the wind to prey at fortune." Poor, deluded tyrant lover. To reclassify Desdemona as a bird of prey unfit for captivity is, I grant, a romantic gesture but his whim never proceeds beyond the hypothetical, and inevitably she falls victim to the worst kind of taming. If only she showed half of N's wild nature! I too must let go. Society would revel in its judgement of me but I have nothing to reproach myself for. I must simply learn to live with love's devastating imprint. The damage wrought by this abrupt exposure, the numb awareness of how I must endure the rest of my life without her as the days and months of her sojourn pass, these things threaten to overwhelm me for she has brought the wide world into my attic cell, conjured oceans from raindrops for me and opened the lid of the sky. What a glorious, glorious thing; I am in love!

25 December 1885 – Darkest

1 am

Three years ago, during an unprovoked marital assault, I experienced significant blood loss, sustained lasting damage to my ribcage, suffered lesions that became polluted and discoloured, received bruises which caused my neck and fingers to swell and distend. All this I would willingly undergo again if it would only restore N to me. In my many musings on the nature of pain, I have only ever dawdled at the distant borders of tonight's agony. Grief, anguish and desolation are profitless terms, they smack of disrespect, jangling notes plucked on a broken string, while every minute I am pitched deeper into blackness now that my sun will never rise again.

He drawled the awful intelligence of their deaths with such unbridled venom that I was stunned. It is only too clear that he has accepted the dubious credibility of sundry eyewitness accounts with unseemly and relieved alacrity but whatever the incoherent circumstances that brought them to our door, I am shamelessly complicit in one which I know to be false. I hold fast to the promise in her last letter; my child will never return to Stonehaven. When he dropped what he referred to smirkingly as a burnt offering into my trembling hands, it was such a squalid inducement to persuasion that I grew momentarily weak with horror. The sorry scorched little effigy is all that remains of the conflagration of our dreams, and it affirms that I shall never be free of this place. Now I realise the correlation between a woman's freedom and her independence because tonight's tragedy means I become at last mistress of my own fate. I refuse to sit and wait for death like Browning's Porphyria. I am reclaiming this narrative and drawing to a premature close its half-told tale. My unhappy ending will seal my daughter's death forever into fiction and thereby release her for good into a new reality.

3:30 am

I am resolved, calmer now and with everything in readiness even though several hours remain until dawn. Against all logic, the heart's paralysis invigorates reason, and I am thinking more clearly than I have for days. I thrill to know that my child will exist unfettered: our two deaths in exchange for her one free life. I shall have achieved what we set out to do, curbing the contours of our story to conceal its untraceable heroine. Despite my public reputation, I am no fool, I know I face a dire future where briefly promise bloomed but I am no longer disconsolate. I have gorged on love's sweetness and will never be hungry again. As for the man I married, he shall rise in the morning to find his bible stands at Ezekiel 11:21 and he must be ready for when the soft whispers of truths well into a baying fit for battle. I will wield Isabella's sword for her, for her and the countless wives trussed by the ties of marriage to cruel Vincentios, sentenced to silence as once I was. My altered perspective prompts me to applaud Ma's shrewdness in going ahead, ever the intrepid adventurer. I understand Father's impatience to join her now. If he were here, I wonder if he could tell me why so many men misjudge the moon as cold and pitiless in their poetry. Tonight, I see in its pale lustre an ally and a keeper of secrets as Lady Mary Montagu did before me; it appears vibrant and warm, a translucent sickle of washed pearl set above the firs, summoning me to partake in its purity and a kind of cleansing. I know I shall be discounted as just another sad lunatic drowned in a sea of the same but my detractors should learn to look closer. Take sand, summarily dismissed for its homogeneity, miles and miles of bland uniformity. However, beyond what is manifest cluster millions and millions of discrete pebbles and shells, all with their own identities, their own dimensions, their own provenances. Never underestimate that which appears ordinary.

Soon the bells of St Mary's shall awaken the faithful to Christmas but before the birds repatriate the apple tree I will be gone, employing the cover of night to hitch a rope around its bough. N knows where she can find me, and I shall never stop waiting. As I buckle the clasp it is as if her arms are closing fast around me. Is it wrong to hope it is her face I see when I step into the air?

From "When I Am Dead, My Dearest"
by Christina Rossetti

When I am dead, my dearest,
Sing no sad songs for me;
Plant thou no roses at my head,
Nor shady cypress tree:
Be the green grass above me
With showers and dewdrops wet;
And if thou wilt, remember
And if thou wilt, forget

Chapter 9
Late Summer 1886, Oxford:
Mr Arthur Barnaby QC,
the Final Casebook

I wish to be unambiguously clear from the outset; I do not intend any part of this manuscript to be circulated, let alone published, until long after my death, that is if this volume should ever come to light at all. The exceptional constituents of this, my last and most notorious case are, of necessity, a potentially maudlin blend of the intimate and the professional, a combination I have taken substantial pains to eschew throughout my long career. I shall not wax sentimental, that would never do but an explanation of my bond (and Tom Belshire's by extension, I suppose) with Professor Hardcastle must preface these pages, if only to validate my fierce motivation for what later transpired.

Tom and I, orphans in all but a legal sense, had encountered each other as boys at Harrow. Our fathers were both overseas, either physically his was a diplomat who, along with his wife lived permanently in Calcutta attached the Imperial Civil Service or emotionally mine an Irish separatist sympathiser embroiled in clashes at Westminster who would never be able to see my birth as anything other than his wife's prima facie murder weapon. It seemed natural, having identified a surrogate brother in the same forlorn circumstances, that we looked out for each other as we steered through the unsettled squalls of our schooldays, and we have remained a singular family ever since. When we went up to Oxford all those years ago, it did not take us long to extend our improvised fraternity to Patch Hardcastle, a doyen in his field even as a young undergraduate and one of life's true princes. An anecdote which best epitomises our connection follows here, just one among so many in what seems with hindsight to have been an Elysian early manhood. The scene might be straight from the pages of a pastoral ode, violet-tinted dusk spilling across the balmy meadows of Christ Church, the three of us replete with college port, supine beneath the spreading oaks and unanimously failing to find hard philosophical evidence for the merits of procrastination. Suddenly I felt a brisk scratch atop my crown and made to brush off what I assumed was a fallen leaf or an intrepid insect. Tom had turned parchment pale and was attempting, somewhat comically, to shuffle away lengthwise like a sloth, goblet upended and mouth agape. Patch though, Patch began a grave and word-perfect recitation in its original Middle English of *The Owl and The Nightingale*, breaking off only to suggest that for the purposes of this version I was the wise old bird prone to gloom if none too abstinent back then while the sunnier Belshire would always balance me out with his irrepressible optimism, if not his courage in this instance. We ribbed poor Tom for years after it but I am sure I would have reacted as he did, had I known that a huge, saucer-eyed barn owl was just then singling me out for its temporary rustic perch. My scalp bled intermittently for two days while Patch expounded a theory that unlike the wise Athena, I was not possessed of a blind side, perfect for a lawyer in training he apostrophised, and consequently there was no need for the animal to get too comfortable. You appreciate the idea; we three rubbed along, we complemented each other, supported each other like the sturdiest of milking stools. When Patch died the trigger was pulled, the final gong sounded, something seismic and catastrophic adjusted itself. It was as if a monumental crack had bisected the sun, or the Atlantic drained away overnight. No earthly panegyric could do justice to the man, so agreeing to prolong our surveillance of his two children seemed the least we could do.

Tom can spot deteriorating cells at thirty paces but pole-axed as we were by our grief, neither of us was a match for the rapid spread of this uncommon cancer: nuptials, incarceration, maltreatment, and a child, whom I have beheld only once, and that relatively recently. Should we have done more? *Could* we have? The wheels were so quickly in motion that perhaps we should not have been surprised when Pauline threw herself under them. Our early intercessions always came to naught; I know better than most that a wife is a husband's unassailable property after all but the day we all staggered out of that lamentable wedding at St Giles, I launched a covert campaign to turn up everything there was to know about Aubrey Tertius Kite, that septic talisman who was laying waste to everything I held dear. When had this lamp of the wicked been lit? To me, the young man's immorality shone gilt-edged like the hems of his ecclesiastical garments and I hardened my reputedly unyielding heart still further from that moment. Unlike Patch, I was never dazzled by the glossy patina of the man's ersatz respectability. I am not known for my pusillanimity, and it remains a source of great chagrin to me that we did not make more of a stand against his insinuation into the family. It was nothing short of sacrilegious how doggedly the churchman's poison wormed its way into Patch's life, as if he had taken a bite out of the rotten apple in one of his fairy tales.

So often we must go backwards so as to make progress, a simple maxim but one which has always reaped rewards for me. Seeking a distinctly crooked needle in the proverbial haystack, I shamelessly petitioned every legal associate, colleague, clerk and usher with whom I had ever crossed paths throughout the length and breadth of the country and just as I was beginning to despair that the bird may too long have flown, a handful of ruffled and bloodied feathers landed on my desk, delivered anonymously via courier from the Midlands. I speak metaphorically of course but little doubt remained following some rudimentary biographical enquiries, and I was as certain as an archaeologist marking out his site that this constituted the wellspring of Kite's violent vocation. It was an ugly and scurrilous story, narrated from deep in the shadows, wreathed in coiling wisps of apocryphal smoke. Its opening charge gave a colourful account of an inhuman thrashing administered by a handsome rogue with steely eyes to a heavily pregnant Kidderminster carpet-maker's daughter but its final statement, eminently more verifiable, recorded its consequence, a perilous premature stillbirth and a swiftly moribund mother, herself but thirteen years of age. No official case to answer, allegedly, but plenty of silence purchased for a fee that would mute a village gossip for a lifetime. I planned to extend my enquiries further and to cross-examine any witnesses still living even as I made no pretence that a jury would consider the fate of these poor unfortunates, worthy of plausible substantiation. As if affluence and credibility make for comfortable bedfellows! The incident was to form the basis of a dossier which grew exponentially into a conclusive character assassination. Perhaps, as Tom so often suggested, it was Kite's fatally warped and over-inflated selfhood that fanned the nascent Faustus in him but a blackguard is a blackguard, plain and simple. Here my temperament aligns me with Samuel Johnson: revenge may well be an act of passion but vengeance, oh, vengeance is all about justice, and that is my province. For a long time as a newly qualified barrister cutting my teeth at Oxford's Court of Assize my cases would often commence with dear old Tom twirling my dusty wig down St Aldate's, swinging his watch chain and chanting maniacally that it was "Time to judge every deed!"

Not anymore. The clocks stopped for both of us the second the college porter announced the arrival of Stonehaven's overwrought housekeeper in my rooms early that black Boxing Day morning. Her lamentations were sufficiently sonorous but her driver, a scrouty spindleshanks who reeked of the stable, could barely articulate his own name, so choked was he by blinding, strident tears. The good woman struggled a long while to find her voice, instead thrusting a neat package, addressed in a familiar and confident hand to Tom and to me, into my grip. Her escort, twisting his cap and blinking his bloodshot eyes like a landed fish, was all apology, speaking in her stead and explaining in broken but respectful tones how the parcel had been secreted in his shed under stacks of horticultural paraphernalia and ever so nearly disregarded. I remember I pulled the collar of my gown around my ears like a child awake in a nightmare hoping the scene could be expunged by wilful evasion but a perfunctory glance identified the writings of our dear girl and a hurried perusal, which I am ashamed to say stoked a womanish blush within me, indicated unequivocally their incendiary nature; the unspoken invitation urged us simply to light the wick and stand well back.

I am unable to reconstruct verbatim Mrs Root's halting narrative as she chronicled the grisly discovery of the previous day but I do remember feeling unaccountably moved by her initial impulse, the posting of her faithful terrier as watchful sentinel while she reconnoitred the scene. No mealy-mouthed euphemisms or fawning niceties from this loyal friend, despite the horrific nature of her disclosure instead, she spluttered how the Missus looked the same as she did every time she settled in to wait for Miss Elinor. Here she cast a stricken look at Mr East, who dropped his face into his hands and stood swaying like a storm-lashed sapling. With tears fairly drenching her bonnet straps she resumed, impatient to be done but keen to eulogise appropriately the mistress she had so clearly loved. And she painted a lyrical picture; serene, unafraid, paused in all her youth and beauty, cosy in her sky-blue cape there she was oscillating gently beneath the apple tree, living despite dead, as if preserved in ice and guarded by her precious black birds. Her recollection, compelling and commiserating in equal measure, soon swelled into a spirited affidavit, a litany of encroaches and injurious behaviours Mrs Kite had suffered at the hands of her husband. She spoke so honestly and with such bold affection of her wrongheaded assumptions when first she stumbled outside into the frosty dawn that I could all too easily concur that Pauline may well have resembled Christ's mother Mary absorbing news of the annunciation, hands clasped in supplication and divine peace written across her countenance. It was just like a goddess' revenge, she concluded enigmatically, sinking into a chair and expelling a long, dismissive breath as if to empty herself completely of her momentous obligation. They stayed just long enough to assure me that the reverend Mr Kite was presently at home and in conference with the Oxford Constabulary should I be interested, dashing out for help when I succumbed at last to my emotions, composure all forgotten, crumpled on the floor bawling and mewling, loud as a cat in a bag.

Of course, it was Tom who had instigated the notion of seconding Nurse Elinor Budden to Kirtham in the first place. He had registered approving reports of her specialism in women's disorders, and it seemed too good an opportunity to place a pair of sympathetic eyes in the Rectory, considering that we were effectively outlawed from it. We had reeled along with the rest of the hospital staff when we heard of her death in the monstrous Christmas Eve train derailment, so it came as a blessing from heaven that Tom was one of the first to learn of her astonishing survival. Her transferral to the Infirmary after a precarious convalescence in the Oxfordshire countryside provided the occasion for him to broach the abhorrent truth about Pauline in person lest she should overhear it or read about it in the papers; I simply could not do it. The still-fresh trauma of the wreck so unexpectedly eclipsed by his calamitous news were twin blows from which she would never fully recover. Always in accord, we had agreed without conference or prejudice to entrust to her sole care the pertinent sections of the journal which more

131

conservative men would have consigned to the fire. I am minded here to mention that while such a species of attachment as that referenced is not in my purview, St John counsels us that love is God-given and besides, who am I to judge? I have often since speculated whether Elinor, until so recently dead to us too, rallied just a little when the diaries found their way to her, bearing as they did their passionate validation of her cure, her great undertaking achieved. She was right all along – Pauline Hardcastle never ran mad, even at her untimely end. But that would be hard to prove, a formidable task, fraught with problems despite our mounting evidence which was soon bolstered by a scientifically impressive agenda from the nurse herself, matching in every detail not just our suspicions but Pauline's own meticulous records. Regarding the 'death' of the Kites' child, the three of us comprised a benign conspiracy, agreeing never to disclose the truth unless it be to get exclusive word to Linus. I would not lie, not this late in my profession, but I could compromise on her 'loss' if conversation required it. If I bore what I considered legitimate reservations concerning her host family, a visit to the coast in early January more than alleviated them and reassured me of an exemplary and discreet dedication that is utterly beyond reproach. Her evident happiness is just what her mother dared to hope it would be.

For so long, we attempted in vain to contact Pauline's younger brother but he remained at sea, the Pacific apparently, on his way to becoming a midshipman, promotion to Lieutenant sure to follow. One heartrendingly blunt telegraphed dispatch a fortnight after the scandal broke confirmed that he comprehended that his sister was no more. After that, nothing. But if there was one casualty in this sorry narrative by whom I was long haunted, even though he remained among the quick, it was the promising young apothecary, Mr Ishir Choudhry. The considerate Mrs Root sent him our way in the dark days immediately after Pauline's death but the poor man was manifestly changed, visibly stooped and still warping under uncompromising remorse, his once bright confidence dulled and his sagging conscience too heavy to bear. He insisted that he would never be able to right his cataclysmic wrong, despite our repeated and ardent absolutions, and the last I heard he had relocated to London to work with the smallpox medics in Deptford, a mortal risk but perhaps the only palliation left open to him. The fact that he had cheated death himself seemed twice tragic; his life-changing collision with truth and its distorted reflection had broken him forever.

Neither Tom nor I have ever seriously contemplated matrimony. I cannot speak for him but my own rationale is heavily influenced by my work. I was among the early advocates of Divorce and Matrimonial Clauses Act back in 1857 and applauded the fact that women were finally able to petition actively for divorce. Of course, the legislation was sluggish, but it was a start. A wife must prove cruelty and adultery in order to achieve her emancipation, and only then if she could afford to pay for it, but at least marriage was being viewed as a lawful contract and not a divine sanction as it had been since before the Middle Ages. For the first time, the idea of annulment was mooted but the plain truth of it remains that matrimonial territory continues to be colonised narrowly and restrictively by members of my own sex and wives are little more than indentured slaves, in my unfashionable opinion. As a prosecutor this can be manna but mounting a defence is nigh on impossible as long as absolute uxorial obedience means, effectively, that a husband can command his wife to walk into his fist. Moreover, accusations of assault within a legal union rarely carry weight – the bonds of marriage will occasionally chafe, we are advised. The supreme difficulty is in authenticating reality long after the fact so as for it to become subject to the law. And there we reach what looks like a cultural impasse. This contentious class of matrimonial case requires incontestable truth and women cannot be trusted. You can appreciate why I so often considered abdicating from the law altogether in a frustrated apoplexy. Even now, it looks like the only way to secure a conviction is to haul the private into the public arena and I did not become a QC in order to languish in an over-crowded boudoir.

So, it was not exactly a revelation to be apprised that none of my esteemed colleagues were prepared to support my pursuit of a marital assault case, especially one in which the petitioner was no longer living. Neither Town nor Gown was interested in such banalities, unless it took the form of a sordid lower-class display of drunken brutality meted out by a perpetrator in the mould of Bill Sykes. Having taken advice, regrouped and consulted with Tom, we switched tactics very early to a goaded suicide (or voluntary manslaughter) and ecclesiastical corruption, a heady coalescence sure to appeal to even the most sensitive of Oxford Pharisees. Our allegations would range from gross perversion, the profane and wilful dereliction of both marital and professional duty to a prolonged, profitable and duplicitous betrayal of trust. Luckily, the exclusive protection offered by 'benefit of clergy' had been dissolved over fifty years ago, and I was seeking the full penalty of the law, the humiliation of defrocking, national disgrace and a custodial sentence. Meanwhile, we had profited by a head start in terms of investigation and witness recruitment, our spirited digging, often in the most uninspiring of holes, had turned up several willing deponents from a cross-section of society. I was counting on the fact that defence witnesses, however august or exalted, would be slow to offer their endorsement given the base nature of case. They would naturally fear dishonour and discredit but in the event, I never anticipated how quickly Kite's supporters would hang him out to dry.

I shall not waste time and resources documenting how long I petitioned for the case to be brought to court. I robustly refute allegations of nepotism, admitting only that the name I have made for myself as a litigator over half a century may have influenced the decision in my favour and if it did, then my life's work has not been in vain. By the time the Judge, understandably reluctant but obviously intrigued, had acquiesced, and a date been earmarked in the calendar, our evidence was compelling and no longer circumstantial. Courtrooms are so often likened to an aviary but on that warm June day, it struck me somewhat pungently as more like Banbury livestock market, a jostling, bellowing human stew of gapers and gagglers convened for a summer spectacle. The front row of the stalls was populated by Kite's blandishing brethren, the names of whom I learned forthwith, among them the rubicund and fleshy Chance sisters, their neighbours the Ipplepens, looking faithfully down their noses, and the full contingent of assorted Bits. The Baronet Dashwood had sent a flagon of wine for the refreshment of the defendant but his physical absence was clearly something of an early discouragement. By the end of the second day, only the

Bishop of Oxford was left, eyes down and one leg tapping nervously on the parquet, increasingly marooned and sweating heavily in the gladiatorial haze. Kite's attorney, young Godfrey Kimblewick, cut a decidedly unimpressive figure. He was of a lymphatic temperament and unlikely ever to attract the attention of one of our great portrait painters, a jug-eared fellow, his sickly child's malnourished frame contrasting comically with prematurely wobbling jowls. He had long, filthy fingernails which were prone to prodding, jerking gestures and a high, squawking giggle over which he appeared to wield little control.

Despite all this, things got underway inauspiciously; the mob favoured the defendant at first, unable to resist a good-looking churchman, apostate or no. He was a handsome devil, with plenty of backing, albeit on paper. I have never quailed in front of a witness box but when persistent low hisses and mutterings of 'for shame' from the on lookers punctuated my opening address, I wondered if we had been overambitious. There were no surprises, the defence's main argument served for its meat madness and its drink disobedience, as 'evidenced' in a post-natal shift that had never healed, manifesting itself in increasingly wild behaviour and worrisome, self-administered injury. Here, Kimblewick gestured extravagantly to Kite who feigned an expression of abject contrition, was a promising young cleric who had unselfishly allowed his wife's campaign of deception to mire him in disrepute. The charismatic reverend lolled through proceedings as if he had wandered into his barber's, dabbing at his cheeks with a succession of gaudy kerchiefs and assuming a tragic mask all the while radiating a smug confidence which enraged me. The whole thing was thoroughly objectionable, despite our eventual success, which is why I include merely a synopsis of our main witnesses and the final, closing statement here. By its end I found myself not just deflated but demoralised. The decision never to practise law again was one of the easiest I have ever made.

Witnesses for the Prosecution
in Order of Appearance

Mrs Phyllis Farley (formerly Mrs Phyllis Chang): wife of Sergeant Richard Farley of the Royal Anglian Regiment, currently residing in Norfolk.

This striking woman was a risk to be sure, but I knew she would press her case zealously and open proceedings in a lively manner, accustomed as she was to gauge her audience before playing to the gallery. She had no fear of censorship and would establish Kite as a man who coerced complicity even while smothering the rules of decency. What we might lose in response to her perceived immorality we might gain back in appreciation of her entertaining and bold inaugural address. She was treated to stoic support from her husband, a swarthy infantryman who did not take his eyes off her for the whole of her testimony and whose hostility towards the defendant was palpable. While she made some admirable efforts to ameliorate her natural speech patterns, she would lapse when over-stimulated into a distinctive idiomatic tirade that would give a Speaker's Corner heckler a run for his money and it was during one of these singular diatribes, directed unswervingly at the reverend not the Judge, that we were informed precisely how often she had 'copped a mouse off him' and been forced to seek medical advice for a cracked cheekbone and a burst eardrum to name just two of the assorted afflictions he had meted out weekly during his two-year extra-marital dalliance with her. The throng jeered and whooped more than once but even they were stunned into stupefied silence when, for her finale, she folded over at a neat 90-degree angle to flourish at the assembly a conspicuous pink bald patch on her crown the size of a large crumpet.

Mr Ezekiel Chang: her son, unemployed and of no fixed abode.

Another gamble but a calculated one, given his mother's relative successes. During our witness preparation, Tom worked out that during his time as acting physician he must have been present at this young man's birth, a difficult forceps delivery if memory served. An ungainly adolescent, frankly an extraordinary human anomaly, he was met with rowdy derision but soon had the company eating out of his hand. The Judge seemed violently disposed to dislike him on sight, a reaction soon clarified by the witness himself as he hollered a breezy salutation and reminisced about several hours spent up his worshipfulness' chimney in the execution of his duties, all on the explicit orders of the reverend Kite, "'im as is sat over there". His was a completely unselfconscious pantomime, the countless often excruciating exposés generating considerable public gratification, despite the Judge's repeated and thunderous commands to limit his remarks exclusively to the specifics of his employer and to report to the bailiff at the end of the day lest there were further charges to answer. The Bishop of Oxford beat a swift retreat during Mr Chang's damning testimony, attempting to re-enter the courtroom surreptitiously only to be greeted with rapturous applause. All in all, a very good start to proceedings.

Miss Clara Pebble: waitress at Miss Muldoon's Muffins and More, Blue Boar Street, Oxford.

Young women in service all too often find themselves accused of incitement in sexual assault allegations and I was relieved that Miss Pebble's tenure as a servant in Kite's Oxford residence was long behind her so as to avoid this grubby presumption. It was evident as she took the stand that she was terrified, but she presented as the image of respectability, however hard her enthusiastic patron, a gigantic female festooned in improbable headgear, tried to catch her eye. Miss Pebble was tentative to start with, concentration so crimping her pointed features that it became painful to watch her but she had rehearsed diligently and her perfect recall of the worst of Mrs Kite's abuses made for a hypnotic deposition, discharged in high, clear tones which lent itself not just to credibility but to esteem. Patently fond of her erstwhile mistress, she never once allowed her words to become adversely affected by emotion or sentimentality; she referred to no notes, took no direction and spoke for nigh on a full half hour all while evincing a cool indifference to her former employer. Tom wept openly throughout her statement and the Judge was forced to call a recess when, during a particularly graphic portrayal, an elderly woman lost consciousness and fainted into the aisle.

Mrs Florence Root: formerly employed as Housekeeper and Cook at Kirtham Rectory, Kirtham, currently residing at Leamington Spa.

Mrs Root had to be coaxed into appearing at all, so riven was she by her experiences under Kite's roof. I had scheduled her evidence to mark the end of what turned out to be a sensational day, and I was mortified to compel her to take the stand in order to further a drama which would have the mob baying for more. In the end, it seemed that her recital of the facts to me the morning after she found Pauline was merely the dress rehearsal of her tour de force performance. The house was treated to the unexpurgated fury of a woman routinely underestimated. By the time the gavel sounded the courtroom was silent as a church as we all hearkened to the protracted scream ringing out above the bells of St Mary's, all touched ice on the victim's dead lashes, all noted the cruel blue of her fingertips. The curtain came down on a fruit tree shrouded in frozen dew and a convocation of clamouring jackdaws grieving in its branches, the last resting place of the beleaguered Mrs Pauline Kite.

Nurse Elinor Budden: employed at the Radcliffe Infirmary, Oxford.

If I recognised a moment when I thought the case might tip our way, it was when Elinor proceeded briskly up the steps into the box. Kite looked just like I imagine Macbeth did on catching sight of Banquo at his dinner table. From then on, his bluster began to dwindle and his face looked on the tinge of a condemned man's. Elinor's professionalism and expertise won over the most cynical of the court's observers and set the grave tone for the second day. She exhibited command, discretion and total conviction, never once straying into the mawkish, or betraying her own heartbreak, building a profile of a controlling marriage in which the husband, a man of God, dispensed pain like absolution, and at every turn there came authentication from reams of documents: scientific terms, dates, descriptions, diagrams. It was relentless and masterly. Kimblewick's cross examination was bruising but Elinor gave as good as she got and by the time she stepped down, the defence was licking its wounds and she was already being feted as having thrown the winning punch.

Dr Frederick Richardson: Dean of St John's College, Oxford.

This was merely a rubber-stamping exercise whereby the Dean effectively dissociated himself, his college, the university and thereby the city decisively from the Reverend Kite, his early appointment as curate he claimed, somewhat cryptically, to have been the result of an administration error. He professed an earnest sympathy for the remaining family of Pauline Kite, whose eminent father was among the most celebrated scholars in the history of the university and to whose unimpeachable character he would attest gladly.

General Sir Antony Amey, Bart., residing at Somerton Grange, Oxfordshire.

Once we had alluded, in camera, to the extensiveness of our findings concerning the Kidderminster affair, it was not too arduous to secure the services of Kite's distinguished relation in some reserved capacity. He was the most difficult witness I have ever instructed, and more than once I recognised in him the same obdurate intractability to which he so objected in his nephew. Fully exploiting his daunting stature and natural belligerence in order to intimidate, his habit of thrusting a lit cigar into his interlocutor's face was one at which even I drew the line. After a day or so of stiff and unyielding dialogue, I got the measure of the man, even if I never learned to like him. We never underestimated how invaluable he was to us and how nearly we had missed our chance. Imminently, he was to take up a post in the British Crown Colony of Bermuda, where he would see out his days and where any stain of dishonour would be washed away each morning by an azure tide. He wanted nothing more than to rid himself forever of the connection with his stepsister's boy, whom he considered both insubordinate and dissolute. We had come to a shrewd arrangement; in return for withholding distinct details concerning the architect of the early compensation scheme the death of the youngster and her baby had demanded, he was all too happy to denounce the wastrel he had long considered a volatile embarrassment to the family. It transpired that his monastic sensibilities found themselves provoked not so much by Kite's taste for aggression as by his carnality. He pronounced himself sickened by the transgressive promiscuity of an ordained man of God. So much for the changed life begotten by a career in the cloth, he vouchsafed gloomily, the bloody libertine had strangled himself with his own dog collar.

Turned out impeccably in regimental togs, he made for a daunting final witness, substantial and erect with bulbous eyes and an angry, froggy glare. He might as well have drawn a hammer from his striped twill trousers and beaten the final nail into Kite's coffin there and then. The Kidderminster case was historical, but the effect in the courtroom immediate. The General first lacerated all ties between himself and the defendant, they were hardly blood relatives after all, and he considered his moral duty to outrank a slender obligation made in a lady's drawing room. Complete annihilation ensued. The Midlands carpet-maker swore that Kite had forced himself on his daughter and should be made to marry her, he boomed in stentorian tones fit for the parade ground. He shrugged off the fact that he had no hard proof, aside from some typically tactless bragging; he had frequently seen the defendant angered and could attest to his methods in the heat of a perceived insult. The Criminal Law Amendment Act, which had raised the female age of consent to 16, had come too late to aid us, but by the time I had finished Aubrey Kite could not but be remembered as a lascivious boor who had raped a child before bolting into a fraudulent calling to save his own skin. The ancillary suggestion that he had been responsible for not one but two unseasonable and harrowing deaths hung in the air like nasty putrefaction. Soon after that, Baronet Dashwood sent word condemning in the fiercest and most scornful terms his former votary, followed expeditiously by the Bishop of Oxford, much chastened and rather red-faced, who advocated immediate laicisation, even before the jury had retired to consider its verdict.

Was it just me who felt our triumph to be something of a hollow anti-climax? I had anticipated that the jury would barely register Pauline's sustained ordeal, mesmerised as it was by the lurid hatchet job playing out before it but still, I felt the need to bring her to the fore of my conclusions. My closing argument, therefore, took advantage of the sombre mood to consider society's current attitudes to suicide. I started by citing Bonser's excellent pamphlet from the year before, a work I much admire to this day. The "Right to Die" demanded of us all two things: the legalisation of the act in certain cases and the long overdue mitigation of the harsh prejudice with which it was commonly regarded. I would eventually petition the court for the right to bury our dear girl alongside her parents but that would come later. This was not hysteria, I argued, this was not an act of melancholy, she was not wilful, she was not fallen, she was not an aberration of feminine nature. The manner of her death was the sole autonomous action remaining to Pauline, unequipped as she was to continue with the lonely brutishness of a sham marriage. If she must be considered a criminal for committing self-murder, the sentence handed to her at the altar had surely been served. Compassion and mercy were required, in line with the great poet Coleridge's claim that hope without an object cannot live.

But I am tired now. I must rest, as the doctors keep insisting. I close with the vehement hope that Kite receives bounteous treatment in his own kind, which is rather unchristian of me, I admit. The wheeling screams of his namesake high above the garden of St John's are scouring the sky like the cry of the damned, exiled forever from the holy sacraments. Not much of a lullaby but it will more than suffice.

From "Remembrance"
by Emily Bronte

No later light has lightened up my heaven,
No second morn has ever shone for me;
All my life's bliss from thy dear life was given,
All my life's bliss is in the grave with thee.
But, when the days of golden dreams had perished,
And even Despair was powerless to destroy,
Then did I learn how existence could be cherished,
Strengthened, and fed without the aid of joy.

Chapter 10
Winter 1899, Lyme Regis:
A Flame Still Burning

The snippet of sky outside his window deepens from lavender to gentian within the space of a minute. As the December day wanes Lyme's favourite eccentric, the bookseller William Vardy, sets about shutting up his shop, plucking stray copies of The Captain from The Anglo-Saxon Review rack, then moving on to wrap rare, signed editions tenderly in their brown paper jackets for stacking safely under the counter. The wind is rising, whipping in off the sea, and the evening is closing in fast. He shudders involuntarily as the first fat flakes of wet snow swirl across Gun Cliff before sweeping into the growing gloom beyond the harbour wall. He is ready for his dinner but must take advantage of the dying light to finish his chores before the first festive nip of damson gin. He sighs quietly to himself, knotting his flimsy, moth-eaten muffler about his skinny throat and pulling on patched yellow mittens before tottering out to secure the latch on the shutters. Troubled waves are soughing wearily into the purpling sky. Lifting his face to the salty air he glimpses a scrap of copper, brilliant against the slate-grey stones of the pier. Squinting through the dusk, his blood is temporarily warmed, and his spirit comforted by this most habitual of sights: stark against the black shingle beach, like a hearth around a single glowing ember, a solitary flame-haired girl. Now he hears her, a low, melodious, mermaid's croon wafted out beyond the breakers by a thickening north wind. He grins, and while he knows she cannot yet see him he raises his fist in salute to the familiar figure. For he is certain of the pose she has adopted, arms flung wide, pale fingers splayed, and a broad smile splitting her face despite the hostile weather. In flashes of amber fire, her tawny hair makes a halo in the dark and as she finally catches sight of him a gobbet of excitement, of sheer joy and hope rises up in his throat like a prayer.

Everyone in Lyme knows Brianna, they have all collaborated on her story. The Buddens took her in no questions asked when Miss Elinor steamed in out of the blue all those years ago. It was December then too and she would return forthwith and this time for good, she promised but she had one more debt to pay, one more mission to accomplish. And the mite was left behind, a scrawny, silent bundle of nothing, a winter-eyed smudge with wet fox pelt hair and a dog's bite tear in her lip. From then on, snug in her bed in Silver Street, Lyme had become her home. Brianna hungered still for stories of the Cobb, its countless renaissances, its solid reassuring all-encompassing embrace. From its impractical origins of smashed wooden casks and mounds of rubble, patched, mended and all but destroyed in the Great Storm of 1824, the distinctive curve of stout black Portland stone had risen again to protect the town from erosion, a refuge for traffic plying the treacherous coastline.

Miss Elinor did come back, much later, as bonny as ever but much less blithe and while everyone kept their counsel it dispersed unspoken sorrow throughout the close-knit community. She had always resembled something resilient from the land, vital and connected to the earth like a hardy windward shrub or a shifted silt bank newly sprung with shoots. On her return, while she seemed unmoored, she was never aimless, her chief distraction custody of the girl, whom she reared in the image of a lioness. These days, the Budden family is all awry. Three years have passed since Pa pushed off to smite the surrounding furrows from the comfort of his own fireside with his daughters ranged around him like seraphim, five since Miss Elinor was last able to wheel him to the shore to scoop saltwater onto his snowy beard. Vardy brushes a hot tear-trickle from his eye as he twists two-handed the key to the heavy shop door and mouths a silent vale to his departed friend. Sad that Pa never saw Miss Harriet married to the Chideock grain merchant. His wedding gift to the school which was saying goodbye to her was enough to build not one but two new chambers, one of them a library, both with sea views and bright window boxes. Miss Flora supervised the construction every day and Vardy has recently made so bold as to place a wager at The Volunteer that she'll be hitched to that Parson Gennifer by Eastertide. Pulling his scruffy coat more narrowly about his shoulders, he can't help but feel nostalgic. There's Mam as can't be left alone, wandering so far in her mind even while she's bound to her chair by the bay window. Miss Elinor ministers to her, quieter, greyer but just as committed as she ever was. One thing's for sure, every one of them had a hand in the child's happy ending.

As he trudges up the lane towards the Butter Market Vardy chuckles aloud in the sparkling dark. Yes, over time, like the tilted skiffs in the harbour Brianna had righted herself with each new tide. Now she considers the cliff circle of hay and moss her home and her nightmares have long been hushed by the susurrations of the waves. He's not to know that sometimes, not so often now, she wakes to a ragged memory, already fading like a bruise, of a pair of bitter, bespectacled, gunmetal eyes glinting hard through the dark. The chapter looked to be drawing to close until a handsome naval officer emerged from the deep, enquiring far and wide about a girl with coral hair. The Buddens had welcomed him warily in, shifting before long and then settling, closing neatly around him like flying birds in formation. Which just goes to show there are no endings, not really, and he should know. Vardy is still as baffled as the rest of his town at the unaccountable metamorphosis, a speechless child transformed into an eloquent word-spinner, her first volume of poetry. Water Words has been commissioned by the Oxford University Press no less and the young lady just sixteen years of age! His contribution, the offer to host a reception in his shop for the Oxford academic, a name like an English county unless he's much mistaken, who will journey south to take charge of the manuscript next week. Out on the Cobb, Brianna dances like a fiery Nereid across the last of the wet black stones, sure-footed and fearless among the hurtles and howls of the herring gulls. In her mind's eye she is already at with Nor at Silver Street, all scarlet and cinnamon among the Christmas merriment, even as her heart carries her past the curling breakers into the gathering night and out to the open sea.

Afterword

I was an English teacher for more than twenty-five years, but I am decidedly no historian, and I must be honest about having taken huge liberties with real facts in this novel. Most significantly perhaps, there really was a terrible and tragic train crash at Hampton Gay in Oxfordshire but it took place on Christmas Eve in 1874. Someone really was rescued and taken to the Boat Inn at Thrupp but she was a child and quickly reunited with her family. I have been hugely creative with the precise direction of the train route and the lines to suit my purposes as well as changing some of the outcomes of the carriages and passengers. But I wanted to use the original as a basis for the story as it marked such a seminal disaster and warrants memorial. Gerard Manley Hopkins really was a curate at the Oxford Oratory in 1877 for a year but the Dominicans at Blackfriars would never have appeared at St Aloysius then because they were suppressed by Henry VIII and did not resurface in Oxford until the 1920s. I hope these historical elasticities don't ruin the story for anyone.

Importantly, the Akeman Benefice still looks after seven Oxfordshire churches and is named after a local Roman Road; the Benefice wasn't formed until the 1990s but the churches do exist, as did Stonehaven and the Mollie Minns legend. The historic old Rectory at Kirtlington in Oxfordshire is where I spent a very happy childhood with my parents and three siblings. The great house in the park is well worth a visit and the Grinling Gibbons panel is extraordinary. There's bound to be more to upset the purist here but I wanted to tell a story with its roots in history; all the errors are mine alone.

At the site of the tiny church in Hampton Gay three stately sycamores, vast and majestic, have joined through time at the base, solid as stone; they gave me the idea for Brianna, Nor and Pauline. Aside from the official dedication, this book is also for Benjamin, "Beloved son of William and Elizabeth Taylor", who perished in the train crash aged just nineteen; his grave is in the churchyard there.

Printed in Great Britain
by Amazon